Death in Disguise

Agatha Christie Investigates

Alison Joseph

CW01095157

CHAPTER ONE

'Oh, go on, it'll be fun.'

'You need cheering up.'

'Agatha, do say yes, there's a darling.'

'It's a theatre show, you can stay in Chelsea, even with dinner you'll be home by eleven…'

The voices rang in her ears. Other people's voices. People wishing only the best for her. Her sister Madge. Carlo, her dear friend and secretary.

'You've been so miserable all these months. Ever since… ever since The Event.'

The Event, they called it. The Event that had no name.

Ever since my husband…

My husband.

Agatha Christie sat in the corner of Fortnum and Mason's restaurant with a pot of tea in front of her. Around her floated quiet conversation, the tinkle of the piano settling gently over the white linen and flowered porcelain, the single pink roses on each table.

Outside, the bustle of Piccadilly, grey and streaked with recent rain.

Divorce. That's the word. The word they all avoid.

The courts had declared it. Decree absolute, they said. Final. Terminal. The ending of my marriage.

I am someone who doesn't have a husband. I have his name, his daughter. But I am not his wife. There is another woman who will take that title.

'…*you need to forget about it.*'

'…*take you out of yourself.*'

'*Patrick is a good friend. And London is beautiful in the spring…*'

'*I've heard good things about that variety show…*'

'…*poor dear Patrick. No one to keep an eye on him all this time…*'

She refilled her teacup. She gazed at her untouched chocolate éclair, the rose in its crystal vase.

My marriage ended long ago, she thought. I know that now. Now, all I have to do is make a decision never to be vulnerable ever again.

She felt overdressed, in her taupe silk evening dress and diamond brooch, her fur stole draped over her chair. She was due to meet Patrick Standbridge, a family friend. She'd known him for years. A quiet, rather reserved man. A widower, an archaeologist, although his digging days were behind him. Now he wrote learned papers in his room at Kings College, and as he said, the nearest he got to digging would be a conference in a nice quiet hotel in Crete. An offer of a ticket to the *Embassy Varieties* seemed rather out of character. 'Vaudeville,' he'd said to her. 'Laughter, magic and music. It will cheer us both up.'

It had been nearly three years since his wife had died. Childless, he had spent those years in unwonted solitude, working on his retirement project, a definitive account of the Hittite civilization in Bronze Age Cilicia. He had become crumpled and disorganized, wearing oddly assorted clothes.

Recently, however, he had seemed more cheerful. She'd bumped into him near Charing Cross not so long ago, which was when he'd suggested this theatre trip. She wondered now whether his sudden interest in the music halls was connected to his cheerfulness. A new, uncharacteristic direction.

Perhaps bereavement did that to you, she thought.

Certainly, loss changes everything.

She took a mouthful of éclair. Her notebook lay on the table, and now she turned over the pages. There were the early notes for the next novel. It was about a legacy, she'd told her publishers. The story will hinge on a Last Will and Testament, which will turn out to be a forgery. Like that case in the newspapers, about those two first cousins who'd taken their dispute to the courts, something about the inheritance of a racehorse stable in Newmarket and a very lucrative stallion.

'*Need to research probate law*,' she'd written in her notes. She'd added a list of characters, their motivations for the killing, suggestions for where it might be set. '*A river...*' she'd written, '*A woman found drowned... A lover scorned... The murderer revealed...*'

The murderer revealed.

'*The plot unfolds like clockwork,*' a recent critic had written of her work. '*Mrs Christie certainly does not cheat her readers, and her readers reward her in turn, but this reader, for one, finds himself wondering why the public is so willing to suspend disbelief when faced with an account of events which, one has to admit, is utterly unlikely.*'

Utterly unlikely.

The words hung in her mind.

But this is fiction, she wanted to say. It is an invention. After all, what would it be like to write a story that reflected reality? There would be no neat ending, no resolution. Just continuance.

Real life. A story where nothing worked out the way you expected, where happy endings were cut short, snatched away from you…

She picked up her pen, turned to an empty page. And what if I were to write a story about something random, catastrophic, unresolved? A story about someone who is just going about their business and then something happens, something they never expected, to change their life irrevocably.

She put down her pen.

Around her, the hum of conversation.

'…my sister was completely infuriated by it, but then she's always been one to take offence…'

'…and then it turned out that he'd known all along and hadn't bothered to tell me, can you imagine?'

The Fortnum's clock chimed the half hour.

'…well, all's well that ends well, I suppose.'

It was time to go. Agatha retrieved her purse from her handbag.

All's well that ends well.

That's what people want. They want an ending. They want things to turn out a particular way. What would be the point of writing anything else? That's the stuff of real life, not stories.

Agatha finished her tea, paid and left.

*

'Agatha! There you are!' Patrick Standbridge got to his feet to greet her, as she walked into the foyer of the Embassy Theatre, which was attached to the Embassy Hotel, just off the Strand. He was long-legged, slightly stooped with thick grey hair. She was pleasantly surprised to see him in a well-cut suit and black tie.

The foyer was all crimson and gold, with a large chandelier. Around them drifted the loud laughter of the crowd, with their crisp black jackets and soft silk gowns. Next to Patrick stood a tall woman all in black, her hair pinned into an auburn swirl, her feet in silver shoes with bows. The woman was standing, waiting, and Agatha realized that she was with Patrick.

'Isabella,' Patrick said. 'This is Mrs Agatha Christie. Mrs Christie, Miss Isabella Maynard,' he said, with a vague wave of introduction. 'Miss Maynard is from New York. She's a dancer,' he said. 'Our mothers were old friends.'

'You're the writer.' Miss Maynard gazed at Agatha with wide green eyes.

Agatha felt the crowd tighten around her. She'd hoped to spend the evening in anonymity, not having to be Mrs Christie, famous writer of murder mysteries. She managed a smile. 'Yes,' she said, as they shook hands.

'I'd love to talk to you about your work,' Isabella went on, in her warm American tones, as Patrick ushered them towards the bar. 'There must be similarities with mine. Although, perhaps differences too.'

The theatre bar was pale pink and silver, with an ornamental clock and shell-shaped wall lamps. Patrick disappeared to find some drinks.

Isabella was speaking again. 'I guess your work is all about following the rules. Whereas mine is to break them.' She led the way through the crowd to a table, arranged three chairs around it, insisted Agatha take a seat.

'Doesn't dance have rules?' Agatha asked as she sat down.

Patrick had reappeared with three cocktail glasses. 'Miss Maynard dances in what one might describe as a freeform style, don't you?'

Isabella leaned back in her chair, one arm stretched out, her voice full of feeling. 'My dance is all about my body. And my body has no rules. The only rule is that there are no rules. I must be free to express the truth of my emotions.'

'I see,' Agatha said.

'Martini,' Patrick said, waving his arm across the glasses.

'Really, I won't—' Agatha began.

'I'll have two in that case,' Isabella laughed. 'And here are the darling cast...'

They were approached by two young women, wafting through the crowd in their direction, giggling.

'Cosmina, darling—'

Agatha watched as she shook her hand, a tall, narrow-faced girl with straight fair hair.

'…and dear Sian…' The second young woman was also slim, with a lively smile and black hair cut short.

Cosmina bent to Patrick, kissed his cheek. Her friend laughed again.

'Have a drink,' Isabella said. 'There's a spare cocktail here, look.'

Sian shook her head. Isabella handed the glass to Cosmina.

Sian nudged her, gently. 'You be careful, kid. You know how it affects you.'

Cosmina laughed, took a sip. 'You'll love the show,' she said. She had a hint of an accent, Agatha noticed. 'Though Georgie's changed the order yet again. Mmm, this is nice.'

Sian giggled. 'We do as we're told, don't we dear?'

Cosmina took another mouthful, then placed the glass on the table. 'And at least your ballet finds favour. Tradition,' she added.

'Tradition is all very well,' Sian flicked a hand through her hair, 'but Georgie knows that it's your Latin stuff that gets the punters in.' She laughed again.

Cosmina gave a little shrug.

Sian turned to the others. 'Our manager, he's quite temperamental. He's always upsetting everyone. In Wales he made the illusionist the chaser, it was terrible, Luca's not forgiven him.'

9

'Ach…' Cosmina tossed her hair. 'Wales was a disaster.'

'So you told me.' Patrick smiled up at Cosmina.

'Cardiff,' Sian said. 'We had an awful time. Everyone got a tummy upset, one of the drapes collapsed mid-show, half the costumes were delivered to the wrong theatre… Stefan said the show was jinxed.'

'He's so superstitious, your young man.' Cosmina laughed.

Patrick smiled. 'Shouldn't you be getting ready?'

Cosmina looked up at the clock. 'Uh huh.' She patted his shoulder. He reached up and held onto her hand. Their eyes met, locked together for a second, before he released his grip.

Agatha watched the two women trip lightly across the floor, still laughing.

'Ballet.' Isabella spoke with feeling. 'Still the mainstay of dance in this country. That's why I have to go it alone. Don't I, Patrick?'

Patrick's gaze was elsewhere, fixed on the door that led through to the stage.

'Patrick?'

'Eh?' He turned back to her.

'My work,' she said. 'The opposite of classical dance.'

'Oh. Yes,' he said.

'Ballet,' she went on, 'it pretends to defy gravity. Whereas me, I work with it. Barefoot. Grounded. That's how I dance. It's not always understood by my audiences, but I know what I believe.' Her gaze followed the two dancers. 'Such good friends,' she said. 'It's been good for Sian, to have a soulmate. She's been rather lonely. Her sister was in the troupe, Madlen, but she got offered work in

America, and of course no one refuses Manhattan.' She smiled. 'I will go back one day, when they're ready to understand my work.' She spoke with a quiet assurance, as she turned to Agatha. 'You must have the same in your work,' she said. 'Wherever it takes you, you must follow.'

Agatha met her eyes. She wondered if she was being mocked, but the gaze that met hers was steady, thoughtful. 'I mean,' Isabella went on, 'however unlikely anything seems in your stories, you yourself must believe it could be true. That must be what your readers respond to.'

Agatha considered this. 'Yes,' she agreed. 'Although...'

'Although what?'

'I have been thinking about writing something more... More real,' she finished, aware it sounded odd.

Isabella smiled. 'Reality,' she said. 'One has to be careful with such things.' She laughed, as the bell rang for the audience to take their seats.

Patrick rose to his feet. 'Ladies—'

He ushered them through the bar, through the gilt-framed inner doors.

*

The theatre felt small and intimate, despite the rows of stalls, the balcony above. Below the red-curtained stage, the orchestra was tuning up.

As they headed down the aisle, a man turned and noticed them. Agatha saw the flash of recognition in his heavy-lidded eyes, as he approached them, portly and moustached, hand outstretched. She braced herself, all ready to thank him, oh, you preferred that one did you, well, of course, I do like the characters…

His hand was outstretched. 'Miss Maynard,' he gushed, as he brushed past Agatha and went to shake the dancer's hand. 'You won't remember me, but I came to see you at the Victoria Palace Theatre. And at the *Piccadilly Varieties* in January too, I was in the front row. I love your work, Miss Maynard. I love your piece called *"Three Machine Studies"*… I think the world of dance has changed, madam, irrevocably. And you are a shining star…'

Isabella Maynard bowed her head, bestowed a gracious smile on her fan as she towered over him. 'Thank you so much,' she said. 'It is wonderful to be…' she fixed him with a dark, emotional gaze… 'Understood,' she finished.

He blushed pink. 'Well… Thank you, madam. Thank you.' He stumbled away. Agatha watched him take his seat next to his wife, similarly large, with chemically red hair and a mouth that seemed set into habitual disapproval.

Isabella gave a shrug. 'Pushing at the boundaries,' she said. 'A voice in the wilderness. And sometimes, just sometimes, I realize that it is all worthwhile.' She rested her hand on Patrick's arm.

They made their way to their seats. Patrick sat in between them, handed Agatha the programme.

Agatha flicked through the list of acts. She wondered at Patrick's life. How long had he known this Isabella woman? Something about their mothers being old friends… Was it Isabella who'd introduced him to this dance company? And then, the way that thin blonde dancer had touched his shoulder, the way he'd not been able to take his eyes from her…

Bereavement, she thought. No one to keep an eye on him. And now, knowing only about Bronze Age Persia, an innocent abroad, he's stumbled into this world of temperament and beauty and people being voices in the wilderness…

She listened to the orchestra tuning up. A dancer, she thought, found dead. My next crime novel. A dancer, tall and auburn-haired, found drowned. A silver shoe, with bows, floating in the shallows.

There would be no shortage of suspects—

The houselights dimmed. There was a hush of expectation.

The curtains rose on a set of painted trees, in which hung bright points of coloured lights. Onto the set walked a dancer, which Agatha realized, after a moment, was Cosmina. Her hair was tightly pinned, and she was wearing a frilled green dress, and shoes which made a clacking noise against the bare stage boards.

The orchestra began to play its opening notes of fiery, Latin American music. Cosmina took up a pose of elegant defiance, as if inhabiting an entirely new character. As she stood, a man leapt from the wings and landed at her side. She gave him her hand, but with a toss of her head that made it seem a challenge, and they began a dance, a flamenco-based, toe-tapping, combative duet.

Agatha glanced at Patrick. He was staring at the stage, leaning slightly forward, his eyes fixed on Cosmina as she circled and stamped around her partner.

Agatha felt a sense of unease. Perhaps it was the heat in the theatre, the packed seats, she thought. Or perhaps it was the awareness that Patrick was out of his depth, that an academic archaeologist, with an orderly life, a slightly shabby house in Highgate piled high with books, had somehow become besotted with a variety dancer from Eastern Europe, enabled by a rather unconvincing old friend from the United States.

On the stage, the dance progressed, with leaps and turns, and now Alexei had lifted Cosmina up and was circling, holding her aloft. The energy crackled between them.

At her side, Patrick seemed to be hardly breathing. Agatha wished she were back home in Chelsea with her notebooks and a nice pot of tea.

CHAPTER TWO

'She can't bear him.'

They were sitting in the bar, Patrick, Isabella and Agatha. The show had been wonderful, they all agreed. Cosmina's flamenco, Sian and Stefan's ballet, a pas-de-deux set to music by Tchaikovsky, a tenor singing arias, Luca Belotti the illusionist managing to make the audience laugh at his failed attempts to saw off his own leg and then gasp with wonder when he appeared to succeed...

'Cosmina and her partner,' Patrick went on, refusing even to name him. 'They hate each other. Absolute murderous hatred,' he said.

Isabella laughed. 'It's often the way. That tinderbox crackle of energy.' She got to her feet. 'I need to stretch my legs,' she said.

Patrick stood up too. 'I'm going to get a drink,' he said. He headed to the crowded bar.

Agatha sat alone. The auditorium doors were open, and just inside, Agatha noticed Isabella, standing in the shadows, deep in conversation with a man. He wore a black tailcoat, and she recognized him as the show's director, the *Varieties* manager, who had taken a bow at the end.

They looked serious, animated. At one point he seemed almost angry, a wave of his hands, as if pleading with her. She turned on her heel, left him standing there, joined Patrick at the bar.

Agatha glanced at her watch. She wondered how soon she could find a taxi to take her back to Chelsea.

There was a sudden flurry of activity. Stage hands ran to and fro, calling to each other, the waiters in the bar seemed pale and nervous, and then several uniformed police officers appeared in the foyer and ran through into the theatre.

Patrick and Isabella joined Agatha at their table, each holding a martini.

'What the devil's going on?' Patrick's gaze was fixed on the auditorium doors.

'There seems to be…' Agatha began, as a police officer appeared, clearing his throat, preparing to address the crowd.

'Ladies and Gentlemen,' he began.

'I knew it.' Patrick was on his feet, white-faced.

'Shhh—' Isabella had taken his hand.

'I'm sorry to interrupt your evening's entertainment,' the police officer said. He was tall, with a genial face and thinning brown hair. 'I'm afraid there's been a serious event backstage. I must ask you all to leave—'

'Cosmina.' Patrick shouted. 'Tell me it isn't true.'

The policeman's eyes settled on Patrick. Around them there was the scrape of chairs, as the crowd began to disperse, subdued, murmuring.

'Excuse me, sir.' The policeman had approached their table. 'You knew her? Cosmina Balan?'

Patrick's face was fixed in a mask of shock. 'She's dead, isn't she?'

The policeman nodded. 'I'm afraid so, sir.'

'How? What?'

The policeman spoke gently. 'Perhaps you and the two ladies would accompany me inside.'

*

The theatre auditorium seemed faded and worn, as if all the colour and glamour had drained away with the crowd. The sidelights glowed in the dusty gloom.

Agatha thought about her Chelsea home, her comfortable bed.

'If you'd come this way, ladies, sir…'

The police officer led them to the side of the stage and through a door.

There was noise, human voices, the creak of scenery, and, somewhere, a quiet sobbing.

'I need an explanation.' Patrick's voice cut through it all.

'I'm sorry, sir, we've only just arrived on the scene ourselves—' The policeman was joined by a fellow officer. '—Inspector,' he added, with a touch of his cap.

'Inspector Joyce,' the newcomer said. He shook Patrick's hand. 'Soho team. And this is Detective Sergeant Byrne. He's told you what we know?'

'Only the lady's name, sir.'

'Cosmina Balan,' the inspector said. 'Found in her dressing room. Strangled. The killer must have struck at some point during the performance this evening.'

'We saw her on stage.' Isabella spoke up. She looked calm, stately and unruffled. 'It must have happened after that.'

The inspector eyed her. 'Yes, madam. The body was still warm, if you'll forgive the unpleasant detail.'

Patrick uttered a cry – of grief, of rage. Isabella placed a hand on his arm, helped him to a stool that was by the wall. 'I told her I'd rescue her,' he murmured. 'I promised her...'

The detective inspector watched him. 'I'm sorry, sir,' he said.

Patrick raised his eyes, blank with shock. 'What happens now?'

The inspector exchanged a glance with his sergeant. 'Ideally...' he began. 'I'd like to keep you here. With your two companions, if you prefer. Perhaps the hotel...' He glanced at his colleague, who tipped his cap and headed purposefully towards the door.

There was still the sound of weeping. Agatha looked across the stage. Sitting on the floor, her back against the plain white-painted wall, was Sian, wearing her tutu. Next to her, on one side, was her dance partner, his arm around her.

On the other side was a motherly blond-haired woman in a blue dress, also pale with shock.

Standing at a distance was Luca Belotti. He was still in make-up, white-faced, with dark-circled eyes and slicked-down black hair. He was holding a ventriloquist's dummy encircled in his arms, and he appeared to be talking to it, whispering against its wax-moulded face.

*

The sergeant returned, and exchanged a few words with his superior. The inspector turned to Agatha.

'We've organized rooms for you all at the hotel. I hope it's not a terrible imposition, but we will need to talk to your friend in the morning, and in all honesty I'm reluctant to let him go.'

Agatha nodded, acquiescent.

She was joined by Patrick and Isabella. A detective constable, a brisk young man in uniform, came and led them next door to the hotel.

The hotel's main hall had a black-and-white tiled floor and an ornate ceiling. Isabella went with the policeman to the reception desk.

Patrick turned to Agatha.

'I knew she was in danger. I said I'd rescue her. She teased me about being a knight in shining armour. I damned well wish I'd been brave enough...'

Isabella reappeared with his room key. She handed it to him, patted his shoulder. 'We'll meet at breakfast, no doubt,' Isabella said. 'And perhaps after that they'll let us get on with our lives.'

*

Agatha was shown to her room by a sweetly smiling young woman in a black maid's uniform.

'I hope this does for you ma'am,' she said. 'It's got the river view at least. You may have to get used to it if you're all stuck here till they catch the murderer. It's like one of those novels, isn't it? Well, I hope you sleep well. Good night, ma'am.'

The door closed behind her.

Agatha sat on the wide, crisply laundered bed. Beyond the window, the lights of the Thames, the illuminated clock of Big Ben against the night sky.

She felt her spirits lift.

No one knows where I am, she thought.

'...*all stuck here till they catch the murderer.*'

A reason to disappear.

There was a small table by the window. I could work here, she thought. I could hide away, from tax affairs and editors, from endless correspondence, from my nosy neighbour across the road who knocks on my door and then goes on about her window boxes.

Divorced, she thought. A single woman. So completely the opposite of anything I intended, for me and for my daughter.

It did not turn out the way I thought it would. I did not expect my husband to want to marry another woman.

She went to the window.

She stared out at the lights on the river, listened to the bustle of the city evening. She thought about her novel, a carefully planned mystery concerning a death, a drowning, an inheritance. She remembered her conversation with Isabella, '*I'm thinking of writing something more real,*' she'd said. And Isabella had urged caution, '*One has to be careful with such things.*'

She recalled the illusionist, Luca Belotti. There had been a gasp at the denouement of his trick, a collective gasp of wonder, a murmured 'how did he do that?' On stage he had been solitary, mournful, childlike, and apparently failing. But at the moment when he appeared to have succeeded, when his severed leg was apparent for all to see – for that moment we all believed it.

Sleight of hand, she thought. Hiding in plain sight. Somehow, we only saw the completed trick when Mr Belotti wished us to, and not before.

She glanced at her notebooks, sitting on the table.

'*Utterly unlikely,*' the critic had said. '*A plot like clockwork.*'

She thought about Mr Belotti's clown persona, the charm of the magician. Perhaps I should talk to Mr Belotti, she thought. As a writer of detective fiction, I have much in common with him.

She gazed out across the Thames.

The moon had risen; the blackness of the river was flecked with silver.

She thought about Isabella, and Patrick; their familiarity and friendship, and Isabella's deep concern.

And Cosmina, with her elfin looks and sinewy strength.

While we all sat there, filled with wonder at the dancing, the magic, the beauty of the singing… While we all applauded and laughed – someone, somewhere backstage, was committing a terrible crime.

She gave a shudder, turned away from the window.

She thought about the touch between Cosmina and Patrick, the brief resting of her delicate fingers against his black jacket.

CHAPTER THREE

'We need one of your detectives, Mrs Christie. That's what we need.' Chief Inspector Joyce sat down heavily at the breakfast table.

Morning sunlight streamed across the hotel restaurant. The starched white cloths, the sparkle of silver tableware seemed to assert that whatever chaos lurked in the theatre next door, at least here there was order and calm.

'That's what we need,' the inspector repeated. 'We need an answer.'

Agatha surveyed the dining area. Around them, the soft hubbub of fellow guests living their ordinary lives. So far there'd been no sign of either Patrick or Isabella.

'I fear it's not so simple,' she said.

'Of course, you'll want to know.'

'Well, I—'

'Dancers, you see,' the policeman said. 'She was twenty-six, poor girl. From Romania, one of those industrial towns there. Cosmina Balan. She seems to have fled from poverty in order to continue her dancing. She met her partner here, Alexei Fyodor Petrovich. They danced so beautifully, but it was no secret they could hardly bear each other. The lads are having a chat with him now. The stagehands say that they heard them having a very loud and angry exchange of words just before they went on last night.' He looked up as Isabella approached the table, then turned back to Agatha. 'It may be all this will be solved more quickly than one of your stories, Mrs Christie.'

'Oh dear, I do hope they let us out soon.' Isabella flung herself into a chair, yawning, theatrically. Her hair was loose, flowing across her shoulders. 'I was hoping to go to the zoological gardens, the insect house.' She turned to Inspector Joyce. 'Moths,' she said. 'I have a passion for them.' She scanned the restaurant in search of staff. 'And you, Mrs Christie. What will you do today? Assuming they release us.'

Agatha turned to Inspector Joyce. 'I was rather hoping to go home,' she said. 'I have work to do—'

'Agatha—' Patrick's voice was loud across the wide space. 'There you are. What is to be done?' He looked haggard, his eyes shadowed with sleeplessness.

'Poor, poor Patrick.' Isabella stroked his arm, as he joined them at the table.

'As you're all here—' Inspector Joyce straightened his shoulders— 'I have to say, sir, we do need to ask you some questions.'

'Me?'

'Well, all of you...' the inspector looked at Agatha, then at Isabella. 'As you were there. And you, Miss Maynard, you seem to know the company, or at least some of them...'

A flicker of annoyance crossed Isabella's face, softened into a smile. 'Of course, Inspector. I'd be happy to help. But first, coffee.' She got to her feet, lithe in her loose trousers, the wide silk stripes of her tunic top. She wandered off. Agatha saw her talking to a waitress.

'Do you mean to say—' Patrick had turned to the inspector. 'Do you mean to say – it's preposterous – that any kind of suspicion—' The colour had risen to his face.

'Not suspicion, sir, not by any means. We already have our theories, between you and me. But we need the help of anyone who might know anything at all about this terrible event...'

Patrick breathed out, his shoulders slumped. 'I see,' he said. 'I see.'

'If I might suggest that after you've breakfasted, the three of you meet me and my staff at the theatre? Shall we say ten o'clock?'

Patrick looked at Agatha.

'Yes,' Agatha said. 'Of course. We'll be there.'

*

At a quarter to ten, Agatha was shown through the stage door of the Embassy Theatre by a young man in blue overalls. 'Nothing but coppers, ma'am,' he said. 'All night long. And us with a show to put on. Mr Georgie hasn't slept a wink, not that you'd know to see him. Cool as an icebox, he is.'

She found herself standing in the wings. The theatre space that last night had been the scene of magic, of castles and trees and lights, was now just plain brick. She was aware of the height stretching away above her, the ropes and rails and sheets of canvas all ready to create their next illusion.

'The smell of the greasepaint—'

25

A woman was crossing the stage towards her. She was blonde, petite, with a sweet, maternal face and a well-cut blue dress. 'The theatre,' she said. 'It gets to you.' She reached out a hand. 'Alicia Nethersall. Costume department.'

Agatha recognized her as the woman who'd been comforting the weeping Sian the night before.

Agatha shook her hand. 'Agatha Christie,' she said.

'Yes.' Miss Nethersall nodded gravely. 'It's to be hoped that the police will do their job and leave us in peace,' she added. 'Isn't it, Hywel,' she said, as a man approached them. He was tall, broad shouldered and hazel eyed, and Agatha realized he was the singer, the Welsh tenor who had sung so beautifully the night before.

'Isn't it what, my dear?' He bestowed a warm, twinkling smile on his friend.

'We hope the police will do their job and go,' she said to him.

'Georgie's furious,' he said. 'He wants them out of his theatre, he keeps saying. Furious at the cancellation. One night only, he says. Tomorrow, we're back on.'

'We are?' Alicia blinked at him.

He nodded. 'Boss's orders,' he said. 'The show must go on.'

'But we're one act down—'

'He's booked a substitute.'

'Already?' Alicia was wide-eyed. 'Who?'

'He's got Saffra the Levitating Queen. You know them, Terry and Gladys Snell.'

'He'll stop at nothing Georgie. He's wanted to book them for months,' she said.

Hywel smiled. 'Nothing like a murder investigation as an opportunity as far as Georgie's concerned.'

Alicia gave a harrumph. 'Well I hope they've got their own costumes. I don't have time to dress anyone new before tomorrow—' She turned as Sian ran across the stage towards them. 'Sian,' she said. 'Whatever is it?'

Sian was wearing a shapeless grey dress and her face was streaked with tears. 'Alexei,' she said. 'He's terrified. He says they're going to arrest him.' She dashed tears from her eyes. 'Stefan says they can't, he says they need more evidence. Someone said there was a row before they went onstage—'

'Just one of their usual rows.' Sian's partner appeared. He was thin, muscular, with short brown hair and a fine-featured face.

'Stefan, you must tell them—' Sian turned to him.

'These police know nothing about the business if they think that's grounds for arrest,' he said. His voice was firm.

'That's true,' Alicia said.

'It was just their way,' Stefan said. 'Just how they'd get into the mood before they went on.'

Sian managed a smile, rested her hand on his arm.

He seemed to soften. 'Sian here has a lost a friend,' he said, turning to Agatha. 'It's the nature of the theatre. We make close friendships very quickly.'

'Inseparable,' Alicia agreed. 'That's how a company forms.'

'And she was loved, Cosmina.' Hywel spoke in warm Welsh tones. 'She hadn't been with us long, but we loved her.'

A silence settled over the group. Then, one by one, they drifted away, Alicia back to her costume rail, Hywel to the dressing rooms, Stefan and Sian to the stage door, he with a protective arm around her shoulders.

The stage was empty. Agatha headed for the staircase. She glanced back, aware of movement, and was surprised to see Patrick, standing in the shadows across the stage. He was gazing upwards at the drape rails. Then he took a few steps to the back wall and grabbed one of the ropes from its hooks, and began to unleash it. The rail creaked downwards, its painted scenery swinging wildly, the fairy castle distorted by the motion. Patrick's gaze was fixed on the rail as it shuddered to stillness. Then, he heaved on the rope and the drape lurched upwards again, back to its place. Patrick looped the rope back to its hook and slipped away.

Way up in the flies, the canvas swung gently. Agatha stared up into the darkness, listening to the soft rhythmic creaking slow to silence.

She went down the stairs.

The noise and chatter of the theatre bar fractured her unease. She wondered at the mid-morning crowd, elbows leaning on the bar, cigarettes between sleepy fingers.

'Agatha.' The warm American tones pierced the hubbub. Isabella was seated on a bar stool, a cup of coffee in front of her. Her hair was now pinned up, and her lipstick matched its auburn sheen. 'I assume you've received word of our darling police inspector?'

Agatha blinked at her. 'I was – I was backstage,' she began.

'He sent a messenger. He's tied up. He'll meet us at the hotel later on today. Something about a fight in a Soho casino at four o'clock this morning.' She shrugged. 'At least I'm free for the day. I've heard that the Zoological Society has acquired a cecropia silkmoth.'

'Ah.' Agatha surveyed the room, the washed-out crowd, the thin sunlight from the window beyond.

'So,' Isabella smiled. 'It rather suits me that Inspector Joyce has summoned us here only to neglect us. I've lost Patrick already. And – between you and me – that's rather convenient. I was hoping to talk to you in confidence.'

She had added a loose navy jacket to her ensemble, with a bright orange silk scarf draped at her neck. She jumped down from the stool, took Agatha by the arm. 'Let's go out to the terrace.'

The morning clouds had lifted. The Embankment sparkled in the spring sunlight. The river was busy with traffic, freight ships pulled by tugboats, sleek sailboats, even a rowing eight, their cox's light, educated tones caught by the wind.

Isabella turned to Agatha. 'I asked Patrick to be honest with you,' she said. 'I told him, he needs friends at times like this. He said he didn't want to burden you. But you have to know – Patrick was having an affair with Cosmina. He's heartbroken.'

Agatha took this in.

Isabella watched the rowing eight disappear upstream. 'I also know,' she went on, 'that there's very bad feeling in the company. Georgie tries to be fair, but he can't help paying some of the

29

performers more than others. The two ballet dancers are leaving soon, apparently, trying their luck in New York. And it's known he favours Alexei too, although they have terrible clashes, major fallings out.'

'I see,' Agatha said. 'And you—'

'Me?'

'Georgie—'

'Oh,' she gave a nervous smile, a shrug. 'Georgie and I – we've crossed paths before. It's a small world, show business.' She turned away, gathered her scarf around her shoulders. She looked back at Agatha. 'The point is – someone must look after Patrick. He's a very kind man. Very kind. As you know. But – I worry that he'll... he really is beside himself. He was just emerging after all that loneliness, after Sylvia's death. And now this. I don't know about you, but as far as I'm concerned, if someone was to take away the person I loved most in the whole world, I'd feel nothing but vengeful rage.' She looked at Agatha. 'I don't suppose you know Patrick well enough to have a view—'

'I have a view on vengeful rage,' Agatha said.

'Oh,' Isabella said, lightly. 'Your books.'

'No,' Agatha said. 'Not my books. My life.'

Isabella looked at her, a question in her eyes. Then, a shrug, a gathering of orange silk. 'Well,' she said. 'I've done my duty. I felt you should know. It's a chilly wind off the river, isn't it? In any case, that's it for me. My darling moths call. I might see you later on.'

They left the terrace. Isabella bade her goodbye. With a swish of the central door, she disappeared out into the street.

Agatha thought about her notebooks upstairs in her hotel room. She wondered when she'd be free to go home. She went out to the foyer. She was surprised to see Patrick, sitting in one corner on a low couch. He seemed to have a pack of cards and was turning over a game of some kind.

'Patience,' he said, looking up, flicking over a card. 'Or as our American cousins call it, Solitaire.'

She sat next to him. 'You don't seem to be doing too well,' she said.

He eyed her. 'You've talked to Isabella.'

'She told me—'

'She told you I was in love with Cosmina?'

'Yes. She did.'

He leaned back in his chair. He looked old, shadowed with weariness. 'It is the truth,' he said.

Agatha waited. She felt a wave of pity for him, although now his face had tightened, reddened, and his voice was suddenly loud.

'The man was never worthy of her,' he said. 'And now he's done this.'

'Alexei?' She was surprised by his vehemence.

'Who else?'

'But—'

'Strangled, the police are saying. Possibly drugged first, they're waiting for their test results. It shows all the signs of a rejected lover.

He was furious with her, just because she refused to love him—' He was shouting now, and Marie at the box office was glancing across at them, with a pout of red lipstick under her severe black fringe.

'Patrick…' Agatha touched his sleeve, and he breathed, quietened.

'How did you meet her?' she asked.

He settled into his chair. 'It was three months ago now. Three perfect months. Agatha, I've never been happier. She made me believe that life was worth living after all. After Sylvia died… it was as if the light had gone out of things. And now…' He leaned forward, his gaze intense. 'But you mustn't think it was a replacement of Sylvia, oh no.' He shook his head. 'Cosmina was like nothing I'd ever known before. So intense, passionate. So beautiful. Her grace, as a dancer… She brought back the joy to life.'

'How did it start?'

His eyes were bright with remembering. 'It was a silly thing. I'd gone to see a collection, a chap with an astonishing number of Bronze Age Cretan oil lamps, up the road here. I'd been there for rather a long time and I was tired, so I went to sit down in St James's Park. February, it was, very chilly. And I was aware of laughter, and there they were, Cosmina and Sian her friend, such good friends they are too… were,' he corrected himself, and the light died from his eyes.

'And we got talking, I think I was lighting my pipe and they asked for a match, and Cosmina and I… Well, I'd never done anything of the sort in my life before, but I suggested we go and have a cup of tea, and Sian made her excuses, she had to get back for a rehearsal, but Cosmina agreed, and—' He focused once more on Agatha, his gaze intense. 'I know people think it's one of those things, I'm a good thirty years older than her, silly old widower looking for love. But she was cultured, interested in what I was interested in. Being from Romania, my excavation work appealed to her. She would listen for hours.' His eyes welled with tears. 'I don't know what I'm going to do without her.' He stacked the cards on the table into a neat pile, picked up the box. 'It's like the story of the Cilician Pyramus. And like all the best ancient tales, it's true.'

He put the pack of cards into his pocket, got to his feet. 'I need a walk. If we're not required to report to the inspector, I might as well pop into the Antiquaries. They're displaying the finds from the Qatna digs.' He offered his arm. 'Would you like to come too? They've found a lion's head, Mycenaean amber, apparently.'

She allowed him to help her up. 'I think I must work,' she said. 'I hope they'll let us go home soon.'

He shrugged. 'As far as I'm concerned, their job is done. Cosmina was frightened of Alexei. She knew they danced well together, but she would say to me, he always wants more. Always wants more. He would get angry with her. It made her life very difficult...' He turned away, passing his hand across his eyes. 'Well,' he said, turning back. 'As I say. A cliché. It doesn't make me feel less alone.'

Out in the street, he shook her hand, then set off towards Aldwych. She watched him go, turned towards the hotel entrance.

Vengeful rage, she thought, climbing the stairs to her room. But when does that lead to murder?

33

An image came into her head, of Isabella in the dim light of the butterfly house, a slash of orange scarf against the glass. The caged moths flitting, darting, and Isabella, poised and cool, absorbed in their silvery dance.

CHAPTER FOUR

Agatha sat at the table in her well-appointed room, her notebook in front of her, a pen in her hand. At her elbow lay a fine white china plate, on which were arranged two smoked salmon sandwiches.

'Lunch, madam,' the maid had said, appearing with the tray. 'As you ordered.'

Now she held the thinly cut brown bread in one hand, and flicked through her notes with the other.

'*Reasons for revenge,*' she'd written. '*A woman who needs to be in control, and who finds she isn't anymore.*'

She took a bite of sandwich.

What if someone really did want to kill a rival?

But wanting to kill, and actually carrying it out...

Is it enough, to be heartbroken?

She leaned back in her chair. The sunshine had lasted into the early afternoon. She looked out at the blue sky, the cheery parasols on the decks of the boats moored on the riverbank.

And if there's no resolution, she thought. What would it be like, to have life stretching ahead, with no meaning, no joy?

The word, again. Divorce.

A final hammer blow, flattening to nothing all those years of hope and promise.

She finished her sandwich, bent to the page, began to write again. There would be rage, yes. There would be the chaos of rejection. But there would also be a resolution, she thought. For all this talk of real life, of stories with no ending, I will stick to what I know, whatever the critics might say. There will be a conclusion, a solution to the mystery, a murderer unmasked—

There was a loud knock at the door.

'Yes?' she turned, as the door edged open. The face that appeared was that of a man, with cropped hair and wide-set brown eyes.

'Madam,' he said, and she recognized him from his accent.

'I am Alexei Fyodor Petrovich.' He stood tall and upright in the doorway, then ventured a step inside. 'I am sorry to trouble you, madam,' he said. 'They tell me where to find you. I hope I do not get in the way of your writing.'

She murmured words of encouragement, closed her notebook, gestured to the armchair.

He sat down. He was wearing dark red, a shirt that hugged his muscular form, loose-fitting trousers. He took a long breath. 'Madam, I don't know who to say these things to. So I think of you. I have a great fear, of police. They will say I killed her. They will say I killed Cosmina.'

She thought about the dance of the night before, their stamping, swirling, defiant grace.

'We fight,' he said. 'All the time, we fight. And yet we dance as one person. This is difficult to explain to police. I know you are an artist. This I explain to you.'

'I see,' she said. 'Do go on. How did you meet her?'

His gaze went to the window, then back to her. 'Up there, Leicester Square. A bar up there. I come from Novgorod, the lowlands, where my father was a priest, in the church, like in the times before. Then, I train in Moscow. I dance, I am happy, but then my father is sent away, I have no one, very poor. No food. I get message from my father, he tells me I must leave. Then nothing. No word. So I walk. I walk for miles. So cold. The wind, it makes your fingers burn. Like fire. No skin...' His words tailed away. He stared at the floor for a while, as if studying the carpet. He looked up. 'Then, I go to America. Big ship, long time on the sea. New York. But not so good.' He shook his head. 'Then, another ship, big ship...' He swayed on his chair to indicate the movement. 'And then, London,' he said, and his face brightened. 'Here, safe. Here, in the bar. Leicester Square. And there they are, the company. Like finding my family. Sian is there, we talk, she tell me about her friend, about her dancing, her need of a partner. And then later I meet Cosmina.' He stopped, breathed. 'And then - Oh, Madam - we dance. How we dance. There is work, there is money. Like I say, like family. But, madam, the fighting. She is selfish, she has a small mind, they say she is narciss... the word – narciss—'

'Narcissistic?'

A firm nod. 'Yes. That. The world spin and she is at the centre. The lighting like this, the dress like that, just so, no, too long, too short...'

'But she could dance,' Agatha said.

He breathed out. 'Yes,' he said. 'She could dance.' He took a packet of cigarettes from his shirt pocket. 'The minute the lights go down, the curtain comes up, the first notes of music… she is transformed. On stage, I only want to be there. Nowhere else. Off stage… I must get away.' He took out a cigarette, tapped it on its box. 'Madam, I have a worry. A big worry. Just before… just before these events – we have a big fight. A big argument. Words are said. Bad words. People hear me.'

'Which words?' Agatha watched the cigarette turning round and round between his long, elegant fingers.

He was suddenly still. He looked at her. 'I say to her – "I wish you were dead." I say it loud. In English.'

He placed the cigarette on the table.

They were silent, gazing at his cigarette. Then Agatha said, 'Words aren't the same as deeds. Wishing someone dead isn't the same as killing them.'

He looked up at her, a flicker of understanding in his eyes. 'You are right, madam,' he said. 'But will the police understand?'

He picked up the cigarette, suddenly decisive. 'Well, what will be will be,' he said. With one swift movement he was on his feet. He put his hand to his chest. 'Art can come from this,' he said. 'Like Lev Nikolayevich Tolstoy. He knew great melancholy, yet on the page it is transformed.' He stepped towards her, made an elaborate bow. 'Madam – I thank you. My fears have retreated.'

The door closed softly behind him.

She opened her notebook.

'*Reasons for revenge*,' she read.

Melancholy, transformed on the page.

Or rage.

My character will challenge her rival. She will stand, steadfast and defiant, in the path of the woman who has stolen her lover. She will say to her, '*If it wasn't for you, I would be happy.*'

'*I wish you were dead,*' she will say.

She looked out of the window. The warmth had brought people outside, enjoying their lunch hours, walking beside the river, their chatter merging with the carriages and birdsong.

She felt as if she was on holiday. She thought of her desk back home in Chelsea. Carlo would have brought post from Sunningdale. It would all be spread out on the desk, ready for her. Editing notes from the publishers, letters from readers, invitations to dinners or to speak at events. There was one she had left unanswered, she remembered, from Wales, Swansea, was it, or Cardiff perhaps; the chairman of some learned society asking if Mrs Christie would do them the honour of addressing their annual meeting…

She would have to decline, politely. Carlo would write, as usual, to let them know that Mrs Christie very rarely agrees to such things. She's very shy, Carlo would always say, when asked. She's a writer, she'd say, in explanation, as if it were obvious that being a writer and being shy went together.

Which of course, they do. Isabella might assert that we have much in common, Agatha thought, but when it comes to walking onto a stage to express the truth of one's emotions, she and I are worlds apart.

She picked up her pen, returned to her notes.

'*A real murder*,' she wrote. '*A tale of jagged edges and broken hearts. Life, love – and the ending of that love.*'

She looked at the words on the page, then closed the book.

It was time to meet Inspector Joyce.

*

In the foyer, a short, rather round man in a black suit and stiff white shirt was bustling to and fro carrying a large board.

'Where should I put it?' he asked her, as if they'd known each other for years.

'Put what?' she said, bewildered.

'A big sign. Saying "*Performance Cancelled*". Where is it to go?'

He continued his fevered pacing. 'Here?' he pointed at the main doorway. 'Or here?' he indicated the theatre bar. 'At least get them to have a drink before they drift away unsatisfied.' He looked at her as if just seeing her. 'I don't believe we've been introduced,' he said. 'You're a friend of Miss Maynard's, apparently.'

Before she could speak, he went on, 'I'm Georgie Carmichael. Impresario. I'm the one attempting to manage all this. And I have to say, spectacularly failing.'

'Mr Carmichael,' she said. 'It's hardly your fault if—'

'Saffra the Persian Queen,' he said. 'I've just succeeded in booking them. And now this. An empty auditorium – they'll never forgive me. And I'm paying them for nothing.' He thumped the board down next to the box office.

'Mr Carmichael,' she said. 'It's upside down.'

He glared at it accusingly. 'So it is.' He turned back to her. 'You're a novelist, so Miss Maynard tells me. Murder stories,' he added. He tightened his tie at his neck. 'How very appropriate. Picking up tips, perhaps?' He flashed her a smile.

'No,' she said. 'I don't work that way.'

He tucked his thumbs under the lapels of his jacket. He had thinning black hair, combed across his head.

He considered her. 'You should write a play,' he said.

'I have thought of it,' she said. 'Although—'

'Exits and entrances,' he said. 'That's all you need.'

'Surely there's more to it than that,' she said.

He smiled at her. 'You'd be surprised. You come onstage. You try and do something. Like open a door. Then, you fail. You fall over, or hit yourself on the door. The audience laughs like billy-oh. You get off. End.'

She smiled.

'Two minutes of perfect drama. And yet the funny thing is,' he went on, 'to get it right takes years of practice. Years.' He bent to the board, frowned at it, turned it the right way up. 'I told the coppers, can't we make it part of the billing. Murder mystery variety show. They didn't see the funny side. And I wasn't even making a joke.' He placed the board by the box office. 'This'll be the ruin of me,' he said. 'It was a pleasure to meet you.' He raised an imaginary hat, then strode away, out to the bar.

*

She went into the theatre. There was a strange quiet about it, and she wondered where everyone was. She climbed the steps onto the stage, and stood there in the centre.

The empty stalls in the dim light seemed hushed with anticipation. What would it be like, she wondered. To stand here, with all those seats filled, with the dazzle of the spotlights. To step forward. To begin to speak.

And what would I say?

I'd have to be someone. Someone with a reason to speak. A character. Not Agatha Christie, a real person, but someone made up, a fictional being.

What would it be like? To search within oneself. To find another character, a different truth.

She gazed outwards, scanning the seats with their anticipatory blankness. She wandered offstage.

In the wings there was a costume rail, draped with all sorts of clothes. She fingered the silks and feathers, imagining how it would be, to don a new persona and walk out there, into the lights.

There was a noise from the stage. She was hidden from view by the scenery. As she peeked out, she saw Luca Belotti. He was alone, tiptoeing across the stage. He was in white face, with arched black eyebrows painted on, and the round red nose of a clown.

He did a few steps of a dance, a joyful twirl, his face illumined with a smile. A small, neat leap – and then the nose fell from his face and bounced across the floor.

His expression changed to sorrow, his body seemed to deflate, as he dragged himself after the nose. He reached out to pick it up, and slowly, with a melancholic grace, reattached it to his face.

And now happiness returned, the exuberant sparkle of the red-nosed clown. In a series of joyful leaps he exited the stage.

*

Agatha found she was smiling. She remembered his audience yesterday, their delight in his illusions, their laughter and applause.

Georgie Carmichael is right, she thought. It is simple. It just takes years to make it so.

Behind her footsteps, a metallic clunk, a murmuring.

'What is the use?' someone was saying.

She turned to see Miss Nethersall arranging the costumes on their rail. 'I may as well pack these back into their trunks. Our London police force might be the best in the world, but they don't understand the world of theatre.' She picked a white tutu from the rail, surveyed it briefly, replaced it. 'And as for him—' She jerked her head towards the stalls.

Patrick had come into the auditorium and was standing, blank-faced, staring at the stage.

'Heartbroken,' Alicia Nethersall said. 'I hardly know the man, but I know heartbreak when I see it.'

Agatha crossed the stage, went down the side steps. He turned, slowly, as she joined him.

'All sham.' He waved an arm towards the stage. 'All illusion.'

'Patrick—'

He stepped up onto the stage. 'Fairy castles.' He pointed to the scenery flats stacked against the walls. 'Happy endings. All make-believe.'

'Patrick—' She followed him back onto the stage. 'We're supposed to be meeting the inspector.'

'What can he tell us that we don't already know?' His voice echoed through the empty theatre. He was fretful, almost on the point of tears. He shook his head. 'Last night I was living an illusion.' His voice was harsh. 'An illusion that life was full of joy and love and laughter.' He gazed upwards, towards the backcloth drapes that hung on rails high above them. 'And then you get up here and find it's just painted canvas and tricks with mirrors. And as for that—' He pointed at one of the canvas drapes, which hung crookedly from its horizontal brass pole. 'Hanging by a thread,' he said.

She could see the two ropes disappearing upwards into the theatre roof.

Alicia was standing by her rail, watching with maternal concern. 'We manage,' she said, gently.

Agatha touched his arm. 'We must find the inspector,' she said. 'And then they'll let us go home.'

'That Russian gangster—' Patrick was still studying the scenery. 'He's taking them for fools.'

'Alexei,' Alicia said. 'They've been questioning him.'

'But they've let him go.' Patrick's tone was incredulous.

Alicia patted his arm. 'Please try to understand, Mr Standbridge. You can say what you like about Georgie, but he chooses the best. And it takes a certain temperament to want to be the best. Highly strung, that's what you'd call it. To get to where he is now, Alexei has had to be very, very determined. He's had a long journey, from poverty to here. He's devoted to his craft, he is.' She hung a Harlequin suit back on the rail. 'Even as we speak,' she said, 'he's out the back, devising a solo dance now he's without a partner. You'll see – as soon as we clear the stage, he'll be here, all on his own, practising and practising. That's what he's like.' She turned to Agatha. 'You must be the same, with your writing. That's a craft too, isn't it? I bet you work and work to get it right.'

'Well—' Agatha began.

'And is your new story another murder mystery?' Alicia said.

Agatha was gazing at the costume rail. 'My new story is about love,' she said. 'And the mistakes people make.'

'It will be a long story, then,' Patrick said. He turned away, descended the side steps, Agatha behind him. Alicia arranged the last costume on the rail and followed.

*

The bar was bright after the darkness of the theatre, but almost empty of people. They all three settled at a table. Patrick patted his pockets. 'My pipe,' he said. 'I put it down back there...' He stumbled to his feet, disappeared back into the theatre.

Alicia surveyed the deserted tables. 'Poor Georgie,' she said. 'It's another blow to the company. The Welsh tour with all its disasters was bad enough.'

'What will he do?'

Alicia laughed. 'Georgie – he'll be fine. He has this knack you see. He's really not at all good at understanding the difference between make-believe and real life. And at times like this it really helps.'

Agatha smiled. 'I can see that,' she said.

'That said, if the company doesn't survive this blow – I might well have to go. A shame,' she said. 'I've been happy with this lot. But I can't afford not to work. I know what it is to be poor, how you end up doing anything for money, anything. I'm not going back to that if I can help it.'

'Back to what, my dear?' The voice was deep, with a Welsh accent.

Alicia's face lit up as he approached their table. 'Hywel,' she said.

'Poverty?' he said. 'You'll never be poor again if I can help it.' He touched her shoulder. 'Have you got a moment to discuss doublet and hose? Assuming we reopen tomorrow, I need to think about how I'm going to look for that Elizabethan song cycle.'

She smiled, got to her feet. 'That stuff is all in the trunks next door.' She turned back to the table. 'I hope the police release you to get on with your writing, Mrs Christie.'

46

They went out to the foyer, Alicia petite and cornflower blue against his wide, comforting stride.

A waiter came at last, and Agatha ordered coffee for two. She thought about Alicia's account of Alexei, his poverty, his determination to dance. She wondered why it had seemed rehearsed.

Her thoughts were interrupted as Patrick reappeared, rather breathless, clutching his pipe. 'Cosmina used to say that if we ever had a life together, she'd buy me lots of pipes in different colours so that I wouldn't keep losing them.' He managed a thin smile as he slumped back in his chair.

The coffee was brought and poured. Agatha was still wondering about this feeling that Alicia was hiding something.

'Hiding,' Patrick said, suddenly, as if voicing her thoughts. 'You're better off with novels,' he said. 'Sitting quietly at your desk, you don't have to put up with everyone pretending to be something they're not.'

She looked at him, concerned.

'Theatre,' he went on. 'Just escape.'

'But Patrick,' she said. 'We want to believe it's true. That's the fun of it—'

'Escape,' he repeated, his tone brittle. He raised his eyes to hers. 'They were bound together by their talents – but he hated her. Hated her. I told her she should get away, I tried to rescue her. She said to me, "But what can you give me? I need to dance."' His eyes blazed at the memory. '"I need to dance," she said to me. And it proved to be the ending of her.' His face was blank, his gaze steely as he spoke. 'I couldn't save her.' He bowed his head, stared into his coffee cup.

They sat in silence. Agatha tried to find some words of comfort, but none came. Patrick looked up again. 'And the police,' he said. 'We heard they were going to arrest him, as indeed they should. And now it turns that all they did was ask him a few questions and let him go, leaving him free to "practise his solo dance" – that's how much he ever cared about Cosmina. As soon as she's no longer with us, he just finds a way to dance alone...' He had turned, and was now staring fixedly at the theatre doors. 'I cannot rest, while that man is free.'

'Patrick – there's nothing to say he did it.'

'Who else?' His eyes were dark with fury.

'All we know is that they had an argument,' Agatha said.

He was still facing the theatre doors. 'Out there on the stage, all by himself, just dancing. That's all he cares about—'

From within came an unearthly scream. A silence, another scream. Then commotion, doors crashing open, people running, shouting – 'An ambulance,' someone yelled in the foyer, 'Quick, for God's sake...'

Alicia was standing in the doorway, shivering with shock. 'It's – he's – Alexei...'

Georgie appeared behind her.

'No breath,' Alicia was murmuring.

Georgie ran to the bartender, shouting, 'Telephone, man, for God's sake – ambulances, now—'

Alicia took Agatha's arm. 'Come,' she said. 'And you,' she said to Patrick.

Georgie led the way.

Agatha was on her feet, following, knowing as she went back into the theatre, what she was going to see. She was aware of Patrick beside her.

The stage was bare, apart from one person. Alexei was lying lifeless on the boards, face white, lips blue, a trickle of red from under his head. The brass scenery rail lay across him where it had fallen, crushing his skull. His eyes were open, empty and unseeing.

Agatha looked back towards Patrick. His gaze was fixed on the dead body, steady, expressionless.

CHAPTER FIVE

'The question is—' Detective Inspector Joyce paced the floor of the green room, a lit cigar between his fingers. It was a shabby, airless space, with rows of ill-assorted chairs and high narrow windows through which were glimpsed blue strips of fading sky. He surveyed the assembled company, then went on, 'The question we have to ask is, had the rail been tampered with?'

A curl of cigar smoke drifted across his gaze.

There were glances between the assembled company. Sian was seated on a moss-green armchair, with Stefan perched on one side. A line of wooden chairs had Alicia, Hywel and Luca side by side. Georgie was slumped on a couch of threadbare red velvet. Now, at the inspector's question, everyone looked at him.

'It was crooked, that batten,' Alicia said. 'We'd remarked on it.'

Georgie turned to the inspector with an exaggerated expression of regret. 'It is, of course, my responsibility, Inspector,' he said. 'We manage with what we're given in theatre, but often we're forced to make terrible compromises.'

Agatha was on one of the wooden chairs, watching the pacing inspector, his detective sergeant standing respectfully behind him. Patrick was sitting next to her, rigid and motionless. She remembered his looping the ropes. She thought of him staring upwards at the brass rail. '*My pipe*,' he'd said, as he'd stumbled back into the theatre, knowing Alexei to be alone.

His face was blank, and she wondered what he was thinking now.

Inspector Joyce paused, mid step. 'It is the case,' he said, 'that we had Mr Petrovich in our sights to arrest for the killing of poor Miss Balan. And now...' he seemed to be thinking as he spoke – 'of course, it might well be the case that this was an accident, an extraordinary chain of events in which Mr Petrovich did indeed kill Miss Balan, and now fate has lent a hand in her revenge.' He faced the company, as if about to take a bow. His cigar had gone out, and he frowned at it.

Georgie spoke with theatrical zeal. 'Inspector, you may indeed be right. Stranger things have happened. And in our world, anything is possible—'

A flurry of footsteps, and the green room door was flung open. 'Darlings – they told me—'

Isabella stood in the doorway, posed in her blue and orange silk as if ready for a photograph. 'How absolutely dreadful. Really, I can't bear it. That poor, poor man...'

The inspector faced her. 'Miss Maynard. Do join us,' he said.

She stepped into the room, draped herself onto an armchair. 'An accident,' she said. 'How terribly ghastly.'

Luca Belotti tilted his head towards her. Sian sat slumped, picking at the frayed green threads of her armchair. Stefan had his arm around her shoulders.

Patrick was looking at Isabella as if trying to recall her name. Once again, Agatha thought about the elaborate patting of his pockets, the search for his pipe; the hatred, the dark fury, the words, '*I couldn't save her.*'

A police constable appeared in the doorway. 'Inspector Joyce, sir – we've finished on the stage. We've moved the – the deceased.'

'Thank you, Officer.' The inspector turned to the company. 'Well, I offer you my thanks and my condolences. We will continue our investigations with the greatest of urgency. And I'm afraid I must insist that you make yourselves available to me and my team in the next few days.'

He went to the door, his sergeant beside him. The company shifted, stirred. The room seemed to breathe again.

Patrick had got to his feet and, taking Agatha's arm, led her out into the corridor. 'Inspector—' he called.

Inspector Joyce turned.

'Surely,' Patrick went on. 'Surely there's no need for us to be kept prisoner here any further. We all have lives to lead. Mrs Christie here has a book to write.'

Inspector Joyce allowed himself a smile. 'Ah, Mrs Christie. Yes, you are free to go. We're doing our duty, keeping an eye on things. Not ruling anything out, of course. But you are all free to go, Professor Standbridge too. Just don't go leaving the country or anything until our investigation is complete.'

'Thank you, Inspector.' Patrick gave a nod of acknowledgement.

Agatha glimpsed Isabella heading out to the foyer area.

The inspector turned to Agatha. 'I fear that real-life crime is always so much more dull than any of your stories, Mrs Christie.'

Patrick had wandered ahead, and was now in conversation with Isabella, framed by the gilt foyer doors.

The inspector went on. 'Here we have one action, a terrible crime committed in a moment of anger. And then, who knows? An accident? Or another impulsive act, a crime of passion, a need for revenge? It's the sort of question I imagine you, in your work, are always raising.'

'Well—'

'If it helps, Mrs Christie...' He leaned towards her with a conspiratorial tone. 'We'd be happy to help with your research. I can't imagine that it happens very often, that you have a ready-made story land at your feet. If you'd like to be part of our investigations, we'd be happy to oblige. The post-mortem on this poor young man's body, for example...'

She shook her head. 'Inspector, it's very kind of you. But it won't be necessary.'

'You mean, what you do is always fiction?'

'Precisely. The story unrolls within my imagination. It has very little connection with real life.'

'Hmmm.' He took a cigar from his pocket and considered it. 'Maybe that's why I don't read murder mysteries,' he said. He glanced at her. 'In my work, the answers tend to be all too obvious. No mystery, no puzzle to solve.'

'Perhaps that's for the best, Inspector,' Agatha said.

'Perhaps it is, Mrs Christie,' he said, as they walked out to the foyer.

*

The foyer seemed drab, abandoned. The evening air outside was humid, its heaviness adding to the sense of things shutting down, closing in.

Agatha went into the theatre.

The police had roped off the stage. A sheet had been placed over the centre where the body had been lying.

Sian was sitting on the edge of the stage, dabbing at her eyes with a large white handkerchief. Stefan was walking to and fro next to her, gazing upwards. 'But how?' he was saying. 'It's too precise. Too coincidental.'

Alicia stood, her hands on her hips, gazing upwards. 'Accidents do happen,' she said.

Hywel shook his head. 'But so soon after Cosmina's death?'

Georgie was pacing in front of the orchestra pit. 'Ruined,' he said. 'One killing is bad enough – we could have survived that. The notoriety might have been helpful for sales. But two... No one will come and see us. I need to talk to the box office.' He strode away down the central aisle.

'That bad luck is still with us,' Stefan said. 'And if that rail really did just come down, very bad luck indeed.'

'You still going on about that gypsy? She was a sham, like most of Porthcawl, in my view.' Hywel took Alicia by the arm. 'Come on. Let's go and find some supper.'

Stefan took Sian's hand. 'I need a drink, love.'

Only Luca Belotti was left, perched on the stage steps. He unfurled himself, a slight figure in tight black leggings and loose white shirt. 'Gypsy curses,' he said, to no one in particular. 'I suppose people have to believe in something.' He turned to Agatha. 'And what do you believe, Signora Christie?'

She wasn't sure what to say, gazing up at him as he stood there.

'Your stories, for example,' he went on. 'Do you believe them to be true?'

'Well,' she began. 'No. In that they're stories.'

'But yes, in that there is a truth about them, perhaps?'

'Perhaps.' She noticed that for all his Italian airs, his accent seemed to be that of a Londoner.

He smiled. 'Young Stefan there, claims he encountered a gypsy, selling her twigs outside our theatre in Porthcawl. And they had words, the result of which was that she uttered some kind of curse upon our company.' He took two neat steps back to the stairs, sat down in one swift move. 'It's not a magic I believe in,' he said.

'So your magic—' she began.

He shrugged. 'It's all technique,' he said. 'Mirrors. Machinery.'

'And yet – the audience – we – were amazed,' she said.

'People want to be fooled,' Luca said. 'It's all in the mechanics. It's just a question of how you hide it.' He jumped to his feet, executed three twirling dance steps. 'It must be the same in your work, Signora Christie.'

'I'm not sure I—'

'Your stories console, they reassure. They tell their readers that everything is going to be all right.'

'It's hardly magic,' she said.

'Allowing people to believe in something that never happened? That's magic all right.'

She smiled. 'Perhaps,' she said.

'And now,' he said. 'Now we've had these terrible unhappinesses. People need magic more than ever.'

'Do you think the company will survive?'

He shrugged. 'Whether it does, whether it doesn't – I will always do my work. I'm planning a solo show, yet another reason for Mr Carmichael to be angry with me.' He smiled. A jump, a slide, and he was sitting on the edge of the stage, swinging his legs. 'This—' he gestured around him – 'this is all I've ever wanted. Even from my childhood, I used to squeeze through the backstage windows to see the illusionist for free.'

'In Italy?'

He shook his head. 'Bermondsey. The Old Star, mostly. My dad was a leather worker. But Reg Slater don't sound as good as Luca Belotti. And anyway, Belotti was the name of my mother's father. She always said it was in my blood, my mother did. Her father, in Parma, used to make theatre with shadow puppets. And before that, way back, they were merdules.'

'Merdules?'

'In Sardinia,' he said. 'It's very powerful magic. Up in the mountains. They have a mask and a whip, and they chase away the devil to protect the sheep.' He gave a childlike smile.

'Real magic,' she said.

He nodded.

'And yet you won't have a gypsy curse?'

He shook his head. 'I know real magic when I see it.'

'And your own work?'

'Ah,' he said. 'My own work is everyday magic. I concentrate on the mechanics. If I leave it to the spirits they may let me down.'

She smiled. 'You just said you don't believe in magic.'

He shook his head. 'What happens here—' he patted the stage – 'that may not be magic. But out there—' He gave an expansive wave of his arm – 'that's altogether different.'

'So you do believe?'

'I am a magician,' he said. 'When I was little, I used to try all sorts of things to make the spirit magic work. Turn round six times, shut my eyes, count to twenty-one, that sort of thing.'

'And now?'

He tilted his head to one side. 'My work is about wonderment,' he said. 'That's what I try to bring to my audience. A sense of the wonder of life. And you,' he said. 'You must be the same.'

'But – my work is in stories.'

'I'm working on a story myself. It will be mime, but it will have a beginning, a middle and an end. Like your work. If you stay around for the next few days you may get to see it. I'm practising bits of it.'

'That would be nice,' she said.

'You can advise me.' He smiled. 'It's work in progress.'

'I'm sure I won't be any use to you at all.'

He hugged his knees to his chest. 'I wouldn't say that. Your work may all be about words. But – telling a tale of murder – you need the silences too. Wouldn't you say?'

She considered this.

He jumped to his feet, took two dancing steps across the stage. 'What people choose to say – what they choose to hide...' He stood, a solitary figure on the stage, illumined only by a shaft of electric light from the wings. 'My work may be about illusions,' he said, 'but like you, I hide the workings. The mirrors, the tricks up my long sleeves...' He did a little mime, shaking something out from his shirt, holding it up to the audience in wonderment. 'Your magic is all in the workings too.'

She smiled.

With a jump he was standing by her side. 'Signora. Shall we go?' He gave a bow, offered her his arm.

She got to her feet. 'Mr Belotti,' she said. 'This company is very troubled.'

He stopped, turned to her. 'If I had anything to say on the matter, I would say it.'

'You have no reason to think that anyone would want Mr Petrovich dead?'

He gave an emphatic shake of his head. 'We are a close company. In our work, you have to be.'

He led the way down the aisle.

Out in the foyer she turned to him once more. He had vanished.

In the bar, she could see Patrick and Isabella sitting with two cocktail glasses in front of them. They seemed to be engaged in an intense conversation, which stopped as she approached. Isabella looked up, with a warm smile. 'Darling Agatha,' she said. 'I guess you'll refuse a martini.'

'I will,' Agatha agreed.

Patrick managed a thin smile. 'At least sit with us, Agatha,' he said. 'We were just discussing our relative freedom now that the detective inspector doesn't need us anymore.'

'Freedom from his cigars,' Isabella said. 'And cheap ones at that. I can go back to my moths. I do miss them so. And here's darling Georgie too. Perhaps he'll want a martini—'

'Not for me, dear heart.' Georgie approached with his waltzing step, all cheerfulness restored. 'We're back in business. Work to do.'

'You are?'

'Tomorrow night,' he said. 'The show will go on. And here you are. Come and join us.' With a flourish, he handed them a ticket each. 'You'll see the lovely Saffra this time. She's unmissable.'

He went on his way, humming a tune.

Isabella gazed at his departing tailcoat. She shook her head. 'Dear Georgie. He's never been one for reality to have much of an impact,' she said. 'You wouldn't have thought all these ghastly events had just occurred in his theatre company.'

Patrick had picked up his glass and was turning it in his hands. 'The show must go on,' he said. His voice was tight, his expression brittle.

Isabella placed her long pale fingers on his sleeve.

'It'll be all right,' she said. 'Everything's going to be all right.'

CHAPTER SIX

It was nice to be home.

Agatha sat at her desk. The afternoon sun flecked the mahogany with gold, shone across the pages of her notebook, the heap of correspondence that Carlo had left for her.

Outside, the Chelsea street was quiet. A gardener watered, the clip of horse's hooves, a motorcar chugged past. Mrs Burdett had been watering her window boxes but had now gone back indoors.

Agatha flicked through the post. A letter from Rosalind at school, where all seemed well. A note from her publisher about spellings for *'our cousins across the Atlantic'*, and did she mind a few changes in the new American edition...

The invitation from Wales, from the Driscoll Institute. It was in Cardiff, it seemed. The talk was on Tuesday.

'A talk?' Mrs Burdett had said last week, calling to ask her what she thought about ranunculuses, 'I mean, they can be pretty, but your geraniums do seem to do so well in this London air...'

'Yes,' Agatha had said. 'In Wales.'

'Wales?' Mrs Burdett pursed her lips. 'No one goes to Wales.'

The title of the talk was *My influences: A life in writing.* Carlo had scribbled across the top, *'I know you hate these things. Happy to decline for you.'*

She picked up her pen.

A brass rail, heavy with its canvas drape, crashing to the floor.

A man's body, sprawled and bleeding. His eyes staring, empty of life.

She remembered how Patrick had reappeared from the theatre with talk of his pipe, how he was always losing them, the need for several of different colours.

He'd been out of breath, she remembered, strangely so for such a small exertion.

But how? How to get something of such weight to land with such precision? It was so unlikely.

And yet, what else? The police were almost bound to conclude that Alexei killed Cosmina, and Patrick killed Alexei.

She leaned back in her chair. She looked out of the window.

The card from the Driscoll Institute was of superior quality, and the bold typeface seemed to exude an unshakeable confidence that the invitation would be accepted.

She imagined taking the train, heading away from London, away from these neat, careful story notes juxtaposed with real tragedy, the chaos of real murder, Patrick's grief and rage, two young people's lives cut short—

There was a loud ring at the doorbell.

When she opened the front door, there was no one there.

An envelope lay on the mat. '*Mrs A. Christie,*' it said, with the address.

She tore open the white paper, saw the signature, '*Isabella Maynard.*'

'*There is much to discuss,*' the note said. '*I shall be in the tea room at Claridges, at four this afternoon. I'd be grateful if you would join me.*'

The street was deserted. Isabella's delivery boy must have been instructed not to wait for a reply.

American confidence, that one issues an instruction and it is simply fulfilled.

She shut the door, staring at Isabella's card, at the looped handwriting, the neat flourishes of black ink.

Or just the deep self-belief that comes from being Miss Isabella Maynard?

She paced the room, thinking. The clock on the mantelpiece chimed the half hour.

She changed her dress, put on her lilac coat and left the house.

*

The tea room was filled with the chink of porcelain and the murmur of conversation.

Isabella was sitting in one corner at a small table. She was wearing white, with a touch of pink, as if chosen to match the tablecloths and tea sets.

Agatha reached the table.

Isabella reached up and grasped her hand. 'Thank you,' she said, with feeling. 'Thank you for coming.'

She seemed different, Agatha thought, joining her at the table, as the waitress arranged a second cup and plate. The self-assurance seemed more brittle, the tousle of her pinned-up hair more careless. When she spoke, her voice was low.

'The game is lost,' she said. 'There seems to be nothing I can do. Patrick – he seems to think – he seems to think he did it.' Isabella's eyes filled with tears.

'But – how?'

Isabella dabbed at her face with the back of her hand. 'He called on me this morning. He said that when the police question him, which they will, he will admit to having adjusted the ropes, knowing that Alexei was alone, underneath the rail.'

'But—'

Isabella met her gaze. 'He was the only person there. Apart from Alexei. And he even showed me a scrape on his hand from loosening the rope.'

The women fell silent.

Alexei killed Cosmina. Patrick killed Alexei.

'Oh, Mrs Christie,' Isabella burst out. She looked tearful and childlike, as if the veneer of performance had been peeled away to reveal this plain, unpainted woman. 'It's so absolutely tragic.'

'It is,' Agatha agreed. They sat in silence, both held by the image of poor Patrick, so educated, so intellectual—

'He's trapped,' Isabella said. 'Trapped in a nightmare brought about by his own passions. I mean, if it was one of your books…'

Agatha interrupted. 'It's nothing to do with my books. This is real life.'

Isabella gave a nod. 'I know. Which, I guess, makes it even worse.'

'Much worse,' Agatha said. 'And in any case,' Agatha said. 'My stories are clockwork, and unlikely. That's the problem,' she added.

'The problem?'

Agatha looked at her. 'I seem to have run out of steam where all that's concerned.'

They fell silent, both listening to the soft surrounding chatter. A waitress brought tea, milk, sugar.

After a moment Isabella looked up. 'It's difficult, isn't it. Finding the story you really want to tell. It's like that with my dance.'

'It is?'

'Patrick is always so helpful when I'm stuck. You wouldn't think to look at him that he would know anything about dance, but he says it's the same as his work. He says it's all about the layers. Digging downwards towards the heart of the matter, occasionally stumbling upon a treasure, dusting it off, carefully bringing it to the surface. He says dance is just a different archaeology.'

Agatha sipped her tea. 'He's a very clever man,' she said.

Isabella raised her eyes. 'Oh, Mrs Christie,' she said. 'What are we going to do?'

'What can we do?'

'Do you think he did it?'

Agatha hesitated.

'When we were all there, with Alexei, dead, before us—' Isabella stopped short.

'He didn't seem surprised,' Agatha said.

Isabella tapped on the table with her manicured fingers. 'I won't have it, Agatha. He's not a murderer. That woman snapped him up at a vulnerable point in his life. He hasn't been thinking straight since Sylvia died.'

'It's true he hated Alexei,' Agatha said.

Isabella's expression was fierce. 'He hated him very much. But you see – Cosmina was bad for him. Very bad. The woman wasn't honest. Where she comes from, they don't know how to be honest. Romania – they serve so many masters, they change their loyalties with the weather. You could hear it in her voice. No fidelity.' She spoke with undisguised rage.

'So – when you'd heard she was dead—'

'I was delighted.' Isabella faced her, all pretence gone.

'But—' Agatha began. 'Would you and Patrick…'

'Be together?' She gave a thin smile. 'Oh, how I've longed for it. I love the man, Agatha.' Her voice shook. 'I love him.' She fiddled with her empty plate, then looked up. 'I tried to tell Patrick, "She's bad for you, she's an opportunist." There was this rumour of a wedding, when they were on the tour in Wales, Georgie let slip about it. I tried to say to Patrick, "If Cosmina and Alexei were secretly married, then you have no chance…"'

'What did he say?'

She looked despondent. 'I fear I made it worse. He said, "If that man has married her..." He was so angry. And I couldn't prove it without asking Alexei straight out. And now it's too late.'

'Would Georgie know?'

She shrugged. 'You never get a straight answer with that man. And it was a disastrous tour, as they all keep saying. Illness, floods. If Alexei and Cosmina ran off to get married, I doubt anyone would have noticed.'

'But – they hated each other.'

Isabella shrugged. 'They wouldn't have let a small thing like that stop them. People get married all the time for ridiculous reasons. It's all much too easy. Thank goodness divorce is just as easy these days.'

Agatha stirred her tea.

Isabella lowered her eyes. 'I'm sorry – I spoke out of turn.'

Agatha managed a small smile. 'From my experience,' she said, 'divorce is extremely difficult.'

'I'm sorry...' Isabella was blushing, and once again Agatha was struck by this new self, this pared-down authenticity. 'You know far more about it than I do. Whereas me – it's just as well no one has ever asked me to marry them,' Isabella went on. 'Because I'd have certainly said yes, and it would have certainly been a very bad idea.'

Agatha looked at her. 'Are you sure?'

'Oh yes. I have absolutely no idea what's good for me. My mother always said so, and it turned out she was right.'

Agatha watched an aproned waitress bustle past with a tray full of pink and yellow cakes.

'That's surely not a very good thing for a mother to say to her own daughter,' she said.

Isabella gave a shrug. 'My mother... Let's just say, I worked out pretty early on that if I looked to my mother for support, or approval, I was bound to be disappointed.'

Agatha studied her. 'How... how awful,' she said.

'Your experience was different?'

'My mother was my best friend,' she said. 'Surely every mother...' she thought of Rosalind, away at school, with a lurch of love, of missing her.

Isabella sighed. 'How do I put this? For my mother, love was a pretty thing, a shallow, happy thing. She was an only child, raised in comfort in one of the old New York families. She was spoilt by devoted aunts, and then adored by all manner of male suitors. My father idolized her. But the kind of love one might have for a child, that requires commitment, steadiness, resolve... I have to say, that was beyond her.'

'And you?'

She sighed. 'You're an astute woman, Mrs Christie.' She spread her hands, palms up. 'Look at me. Following dear Patrick around, lovesick and hopeless. When I know, in my heart, that he will never love me. A woman like you, you have more sense than I do.'

'Miss Maynard – my husband chose another woman.'

'Sure,' Isabella said. 'I know that. The world knows that. But you are a steadfast person. Out there, there's another man for you, one who will make you happy for the rest of your life – and there's no point you shaking your head like that, Mrs Christie-'

'I cannot agree with you.' Agatha smiled at her. 'I cannot see how I could ever marry again.'

'You are an Englishwoman. You are someone with all the attributes of a good wife.'

'That's very kind of you. But in fact, I have spent these months reassessing my life. I've been protected by having a husband. Now, I have to accept that life requires me to accept these challenges. To be more outgoing, as the single woman that I now am. But how? Everything I've ever done, I've done as a wife, as Mrs Christie, wife of Mr Christie. Buying a house, selling a house, going on holiday… How could I do something like travel on a boat, or a train, all on my own?' She stopped, breathing hard, aware that she had said far more than she intended.

'Mrs Christie…' Isabella leaned towards her. 'You are a strong person. Anyone can see that about you. I raise my hat to you, for having come this far. And, who's to say what will arise? In my view, you will succeed at being alone, at doing things like going on holiday, and who knows? You could meet the love of your life on this holiday—'

Agatha shook her head. 'I have already met, and lost, the love of my life.'

Isabella glanced at her, at the tension in her voice. 'All I know is, Mrs Christie, that I am ill-equipped for such things. I am destined to love unrequitedly. But what you must know about me, Mrs Christie, is that yearning is good for my work. A reaching out for something unattainable is always a good starting point, I find.'

Agatha thought about her new novel, the scribbled notes, the lists of characters. 'Unattainable…' she murmured.

'Dance,' Isabella said, emphatically. 'There's the stage, the space, the costume… and then the music begins… and I feel it here—' She placed her hand on her chest – 'and what I'm expressing is something unresolved, something that aspires to completion. That's at the heart of my dance. At the heart of my work. Perhaps it's at the heart of all work such as mine. Or yours.' She picked up her empty tea cup, replaced it on its saucer. 'The truth is, since I fell in love with Patrick, my dancing has got much, much better.' She looked at her watch. 'And talking of Patrick, we all have tickets for tonight's show. Patrick claims he'll meet me there. If we're going to save him from his fate, we'd best get going.'

*

They were greeted in the theatre foyer by Georgie, gleeful and excitable. 'I should never have let you have those comps.' He danced from foot to foot. 'We've had queues at the box office. I fear it's notoriety, ever since the newspapers got hold of the story. "*Double Killing in Theatreland*",' he laughed. 'At least dear Saffra has decided she'll go on. We've had all sorts of temperament from her today.'

Isabella was distracted, her gaze on the doors where the audience was now filing in, chattering, animated.

'So much for Stefan and his gypsy curses,' Georgie smiled. 'It was nothing to do with floods or illnesses. It was just that they lost Madlen the trapeze act. She'd been one of the main draws. No wonder the Americans snapped her up. I gather she's doing famously there – Isabella darling, do stop fretting—'

'Where is Patrick?' Her voice was anxious.

'Perhaps PC Plod has already locked him up.' Georgie was scanning the entrance.

'It's not a joke, Georgie.' Isabella faced him.

'Darling, no one is taking it more seriously than me.' He laid his hand on her arm, suddenly serious. 'I'm the one who's had all the boys in blue scurrying about all day. I ended up saying to them, "If you had any sense, you'd mock up the moment of death. Find a wax dummy, let the rail fall again." Then they could see what really happened. I offered to do it for them, I said our Belotti could lend us his dummy.'

Isabella looked at him, wide-eyed. 'Surely not?'

'The coppers expressed interest. But then Belotti said he'd kill me if I so much as laid a finger on dear Paco. And I have no doubt he meant it too.'

Isabella was scanning the crowd once again. 'It really is a full house,' she said.

'I told you so. We're on the path to great success. So much for bad luck. And in any case, it can't be true. No self-respecting gypsy

71

would dream of setting foot in Porthcawl. And look, here's Patrick. All spruced up and ready for a grand night out.'

Isabella jumped to her feet and went to greet him. Georgie followed her with his eyes.

'Mr Carmichael.' Agatha addressed him. 'Speaking of motives for murder—'

He turned to her. 'There is the possibility,' she went on, 'that Alexei and Cosmina got married in Cardiff.' He said nothing, so she continued, 'If Cosmina and Alexei really were a married couple, it does raise the stakes a bit.'

He breathed, then spoke. 'I heard rumours,' he said. 'There was certainly a day when he vanished. They both vanished. And they came back together, in time for the evening show, arm in arm, giggling like happy lovers. Not that it lasted. But you see, it seems very unlikely. They hadn't been in the country long – would the Cardiff register office give them permission to marry? I did mean to ask him about it, as their welfare was of course my concern – but now it's too late. And you know, it might just have been silly company gossip…' His eyes had travelled to the doorway again. 'Look at her,' he said. 'She really will stop at nothing.'

Isabella was standing with her arm across the doorway, as if to corner Patrick. They were having an intense conversation.

Georgie shook his head. 'She is so determined to get her man.'

'That's not what she said to me.'

'She won't admit it. She is unstoppable. I've seen her before when she's in love – ooh, there's the bell. Time to take your seats.'

72

Isabella had taken Patrick by the arm and was now leading him into the auditorium. Agatha turned to join them.

'Enjoy the show, Mrs Christie. It must make a change from thinking up new ways of killing people.' He raised his imaginary hat, and then drifted away into the crowd.

Patrick whispered a good evening to Agatha, as she took her place next to him. The chatter of the packed theatre faded to a hush as the lights went down.

CHAPTER SEVEN

Afterwards, in the bar, Agatha had to admit that it had been a perfect evening's entertainment. They'd laughed, they'd clapped, they'd sat entranced by the dancing. They'd marvelled at Saffra as she appeared to float several feet up in the air, a vision of turquoise scarves and jewelled slippers.

'True professionals,' Isabella said, stirring her martini, as they found three bar stools in one corner. 'They've lost two of their key performers, they're in grief at these awful deaths, they've got the police everywhere – and they've produced a show like that. It's typical Georgie,' she said, with a smile. 'And you can't see the join,' she went on.

It was true. Sian and Stefan had added a second dance number to their set, a flamenco number, a counterbalance to the ballet. It made the most of their strengths, with Sian's stately height and Stefan's neat precision. Hywel had added to his repertoire too, folk songs to balance with the opera, two of them in Welsh.

'And as for the mime,' Isabella said. 'It was in the tradition of great Italian clowning,' she said.

'Luca Belotti,' Patrick said. 'Cosmina always spoke well of him.' He was gazing around the bar, his face taut and anxious.

Luca's new act had been set against a cityscape, its jagged towers of skyscrapers suggesting New York. The backdrop was all in black and white. The orchestra had played a discordant, modernist piece. Luca had appeared with an accordion, red-nosed and jaunty. He had danced hither and thither, attempting to join in the music with his accordion. But every attempt to play was thwarted, by the accordion malfunctioning, by his coat getting in the way, his nose coming loose. And the audience had laughed.

At the end, the music finished. He was left in silence, still and alone, a melancholic silhouette against the Manhattan skyline. The lights had gone to blackout.

'...Stravinsky-esque,' Patrick was saying. 'The essential alienation of the individual in the industrial landscape. The music was perfectly chosen. And Hywel's set too, those Butterworth songs. Such poignant words about the loss of life in the war.'

Isabella murmured in agreement, her hand resting on his sleeve.

Agatha thought about yearning, and what Isabella had said about her dancing being better for unrequited love.

She felt suddenly tired, wondered about finding a taxi back to Chelsea. But now here was Georgie, full of high spirits, 'Best audience we've had all season – and we're booked out for the rest of the month. I've got half the West End queueing up for us...'

Patrick had reached out a hand, was thanking Georgie for the tickets, 'No doubt we'll see you soon...'

Isabella was asking him how he was getting back. 'I'll stay at the club,' he said. 'It's only up the road...'

Agatha was standing now, gathering her coat, yawning—

The doors burst open. Agatha saw blue uniforms, men standing in a military formation, and then there was Inspector Joyce himself.

'Now what?' Isabella managed to say, before they were aware that it was their table the police were approaching, their table that was suddenly surrounded – and Patrick was being helped to his feet by Inspector Byrne himself.

'Professor Standbridge,' the inspector said. 'I am afraid you are under arrest, charged with the murder of Mr Alexei Petrovich.'

Patrick seemed much taller than the officers who now flanked him, one at each arm. He stood, calm, broad-shouldered, acquiescent.

'Officers,' Isabella was on her feet. 'This is preposterous. You cannot possibly have any evidence against this man—'

'Madam.' Inspector Joyce faced her. 'I fear the evidence is all too clear.'

'Patrick—' Isabella turned to him, as if waiting for him to protest, to defend himself. 'Patrick—'

He shook his head. 'Isabella,' he said. 'I fear history must take its course.' He was pale with shock but still strangely accepting, as the officers handed him his coat and prepared to lead him away.

Isabella was at his side. They marched him out of the doors, into the street. Agatha followed, aware of the gaping stares of the public in the bar.

Isabella was now fretful, flapping between the policemen. 'Officers, you can't possibly act this way—'

Patrick flashed a look of pleading at Agatha.

Agatha took Isabella by the arm. 'I think we have no choice,' she said, 'other than to let things take their course.'

'But he's innocent,' Isabella said.

'In that case,' Agatha said, 'the police will establish the facts and Patrick will be released.'

An Austin Twelve was parked outside the hotel. Patrick allowed himself to be led to it, bent down to climb inside. They watched as it drove away, joining the carriages and motorcars on the busy street.

*

'So,' came a quiet voice at Agatha's side. 'Alexei killed Cosmina, and Professor Standbridge killed Alexei.' It was Alicia who was speaking. 'Like all the old stories,' she went on. 'Love, and revenge.'

She stood watching the jostling crowds of the London evening. One by one the company stumbled outside to join her.

'And don't go on about gypsy curses,' Alicia said, her voice suddenly sharp, as Stefan approached.

He shook his head. 'I weren't going to,' he said. 'This is beyond all that. That poor man. Did you see his face, being driven away by the law?'

Sian was pacing the pavement. Stefan went to her, led her to the steps, put a coat around her shoulders.

Hywel was at Alicia's side. 'Georgie's still indoors,' he said. 'Not a care in the world.' He gestured with his thumb towards the theatre. 'He's counting the box office takings and talking to Terry and Gladys about how to improve their Floating Queen.'

'"Resilient, we theatre people." Is that what he's saying?' Stefan gave a mirthless smile. '"The show must go on." Don't tell me.'

Alicia patted Stefan's arm. 'Georgie only understands theatre,' she said. 'He doesn't understand real life.'

'You're telling me,' Stefan said. 'It makes me angry. Like in Wales – he behaved as if it was all a game. People needed looking after, and all he did was dance around as if he owned the place and then pick fights with people.'

Hywel smiled. 'Not quite fights.'

'Oh,' Alicia sighed. 'You were very brave. You and Stefan here.' She turned to Agatha. 'It was Alexei. He took an afternoon off, it's not as if he was even needed, he was trying to sort out where he might live in London, I think – and Georgie took exception. For no reason at all.'

'Trying to show us who was boss,' Stefan said. 'It got completely out of hand. Georgie just went for him, fists at the ready—'

'Alexei grabbed one of the carpenter's tools,' Alicia said. 'He was waving it around, and then luckily Stefan here stepped in.'

'We both did,' Stefan said. 'Me and Hywel.'

Alicia was gazing up at Hywel. 'Stepped in, between Alexei and Georgie. Calmed Alexei down, got the screwdriver off him. Cosmina had run off, so upset, though she was such a shy girl in any case, poor kid.' Alicia gave a little shudder. 'It was so upsetting. Alexei still spitting fire and fury about Georgie, Georgie looking at him like he wanted to kill him, and these two boys keeping them apart…'

Hywel shook his head. 'In the end I had to say to Georgie, did he want a show that night or not? That calmed him down. He was going on about being lied to, about these shifty Russians never telling the truth, and I said to him, that's no reason to risk the box office.' He smiled.

'And so they went their separate ways, and we all stumbled back to our lodgings, back to lovely Mrs Parry. Dear Mrs Parry, eh, Sian?'

Sian was standing next to Stefan. She looked thin and pale, shivering in the chill evening air. 'Mrs Parry. We'd known her for years, me and Madlen. When we knew we'd be in Penarth, we told Georgie we must stay with Janet Parry. And he agreed, probably just because of her generous rates.' She gave a small smile. 'She was like an auntie to us.'

'She calmed everyone down, made us all tea, got us all sorted out,' Alicia said.

'And the show went on,' Hywel said.

The company breathed, shifted. 'And all Georgie said,' Alicia went on, after a moment, 'when he was watching Alexei and Cosmina from the wings, was how they always dance better after a fight.' She shook her head, disbelieving. 'An unlucky show.' She looked at Stefan. 'But I loved Wales. I'd go back in a flash. And dear Mrs Parry. I loved her too. Her and her stories.'

'She never shut up,' Hywel smiled.

'She was always like that,' Sian said.

'All about her cousins. And her residents, all in the business, whippets who could count and parrots trained to recite the sonnets. And all of it was true.'

Hywel laughed. 'Nearly all of it,' he said.

'I kept her address.' She pulled out a card, showed it to Agatha. 'Always meant to go back.'

'It was a home from home for Sian here,' Stefan said. 'You were missing your sister so much.'

Sian gave a shy smile. 'We'd never been apart. I still miss her.'

'She's coming back,' Stefan said, turning to the others.

'She is?' Alicia looked surprised. 'I thought it was all going so well there.'

'Just for a visit,' Sian said. 'All that way on the boat. We might even take some time to visit Penarth again.'

Agatha was holding the card. '*Mrs Janet Parry. The Plymouth Arms Guest House*,' she read.

Alicia tapped the card. 'She made the best tea in Britain, proper strong, it was, nice and dark – and only fifteen minutes to Cardiff on the train...'

Hywel stroked Alicia's hair. 'When we go back to Wales, we won't go there. We'll go to Nant Francon where my people are from. The slate quarries, where my father worked. That's the true Wales.' He led her away, into the London night. Sian and Stefan too drifted back into the theatre.

Isabella had been sitting on the wall, and now she got up, stretching theatrically. 'I shall be there for him,' she said. 'Someone

80

must give him hope.' She gathered her fur around her shoulders, went back into the theatre.

*

Agatha sat in a taxi. The London night unfurled past the windows, the bright lights of theatreland, the dark sky beyond, the blackness of the Thames as she crossed the river.

Patrick would be in a police cell by now, she thought. She felt a pang of concern, at the thought of that vulnerable, shambling man having to manage accusations of murder. Isabella was so certain of his innocence, she thought, and it was a certainty she herself was inclined to share. And yet...

The rail, the rope, the timing. And more than that, the expression on his face at the arrival of the police.

He had looked like a guilty man.

She thought about Isabella, the glimpses of urgent conversations with Georgie, with Patrick. What else does she know, Agatha wondered.

Alexei killed Cosmina. And Patrick killed Alexei. However unlikely, however much it was like '*something from one of your murder stories, Mrs Christie...*'

In her mind, the red-nosed clown, the painted backdrop of the New York skyline, stylized into angular black and white.

In her mind, her notebooks waiting on her desk, for the story she would tell.

*

Sunday morning in Chelsea was alive with church bells and the scent of fresh bread.

Agatha was writing. A woman, alone in an unnamed city. Towering skyscrapers, the alienation that Patrick had described, the individual in the industrial world. There would be heartbreak. There would be a dancer, an attempt to write into words an art form that has its heart in silence.

She put down her pen. She saw in her mind the red-nosed clown, alone in an urban setting of black and white; she heard the discordant music of his syncopated dance.

She thought of Patrick, alone in a cell, resigned; relieved, almost.

It made no sense.

On her desk was the card. *'Plymouth Arms Guest House'*. For some reason she'd ended up with it, after Alicia had taken it from her bag and shown it to her.

Next to it lay the invitation speak at the Driscoll Institute; the note she'd written to Carlo. *'Tell them I shall be delighted to accept.'*

It was in two days' time. On Tuesday, she thought, I shall get the train to Cardiff.

CHAPTER EIGHT

The thundering blackness of the railway tunnel gave way to smoky white as the train steamed westwards.

Agatha looked out of the window, at the rolling green fields of the English countryside.

Carlo had telephoned Mrs Rees to accept the invitation. 'I apologized for the short notice,' Carlo said to Agatha.

'Did she mind?' Agatha asked.

'To be honest,' Carlo said, with a tone of disapproval, 'she seemed to have assumed you were coming. She'd already printed the programmes, she said.'

The train rattled, whistled.

Agatha felt her spirits lift. Once again, she thought about her need to escape.

Isabella's wrong, she thought. It's not that I should meet another man. It's that I should learn to be alone.

'*The love of your life*,' Isabella had said.

And what if that person is someone you've had to leave behind?

'They'll meet you at Cardiff station,' Carlo had said. 'They've booked you a hotel. Let's hope it's a nice one.'

Agatha leaned her head against the window. She thought about what Isabella had said, about yearning for a lost love being good for one's art.

I could write the story. The lone woman in the cityscape. The modernist tale of alienation.

But how to inhabit that character? How to find the truth of her? A strong, solitary woman who doesn't mind being on her own, who can make travelling plans as a single person, who doesn't fear the looks of strangers, who doesn't feel a tightening anxiety at the anticipation of having to say that word. *Divorce.*

How to write a woman who once was married and now is not. And is happy with things as they are.

She pictured Isabella in her loose tailored silks and her floating auburn hair. She imagined her staring at glass cases, her gaze fixed on the fluttering rainbow beauty of her moths. There is no doubt, for her, a kind of joy in her unrequited love, in her embracing of her essential solitude. She had spoken of her yearning, of how her work is expressing something unresolved, something aspiring to completion. '*Perhaps that's true of all work,*' she'd said.

But is it true of a story told as clockwork, with a plot, a mystery, a twist?

Agatha leaned back in her seat. She surveyed the passing scenery, thinking about the gap between the freeform heartfelt self-expression of an Isabella and the carefully ordered storytelling of a detective novelist.

What would it be like, to be like Isabella?

On the seat next to her was a discarded local newspaper. She flicked through it.

'*The Problem of Distressed Areas*,' she read. She turned the pages of the thin paper. There was a photograph of a line of women, all in a queue, having heard that there was a job going at the local library in Cardiff. One job. About fifty women, all in their Sunday best.

She turned the page.

Another photograph. The majesty of Dowlais steelworks, now closed. '*Something will be done*,' the King had said. The King himself, she thought. The report was written in hushed tones of respect.

It was a beautiful photograph. The dark solitary curves of the factory buildings, against the Welsh mist.

She flicked through the advertisements. '*Variety.*' The heading caught her eye.

'*The Alhambra*,' she read. '*The Caliph of Baghdad, Illusionist. The Bentley Boys. Billy the Bicycling Cockatoo.*'

Agatha smiled to herself, wondering how long it would be before Georgie booked Billy the Bicycling Cockatoo.

The sun had gone in. The countryside looked greyer, leaner. She thought about people queueing for work, a lowering mist of poverty in black and white.

Perhaps, rather than thinking about Isabella and her yearning for elusive love, I should think about Mr Belotti and his solitary clown. And yet his clown is not alone, as his time onstage is shared directly with his laughing, wondering audience, a moment of joy in their difficult lives. Joy, and hope and wonder.

And therein, she thought, are the beginnings of my novel. The city skyscrapers, the spotlights holding in their beams, the lone clown who tells his story to his audience; a beginning, a middle and an end all conveyed in the gaps and in the silences.

The train rumbled through the countryside, leaving its trail of steam against the damp green backdrop.

Patrick had allowed a rope to come undone, and a rail to crash to earth in such a way as to kill his rival in love, and avenge the death of the woman he adored. More than that, Patrick seemed to be accepting that this was what had happened.

She had a sense of something beyond her reach.

*

'Ah, Mrs Christie, there you are.'

The woman approaching her was large and round, in a pale green hat and a shapeless raincoat, which given the threatening clouds was probably sensible.

She held out her hand. 'Mrs Rees,' she said. 'Mrs Olwen Rees.'

'Pleased to meet you.' Agatha took in the neat grey curls, the button-blue eyes.

'We're so pleased you're coming to talk to us this evening,' Mrs Rees went on. 'I told the committee, she's the one that writes those books, you know, where there's a vicar and then the colonel or someone is found dead, in the library or somewhere, poisoned usually, isn't it? And it's always a surprise – ah, there he is, my husband is driving us.'

Agatha was led to a waiting car. In the driver's seat she could see broad shoulders and a thatch of black hair.

'Here she is, Robert,' her new acquaintance announced. 'Mrs Agatha Christie.'

The broad shoulders part-turned towards her, waved a hand in greeting. 'Pleased to meet you, Mrs Christie,' he said. 'Our chairman took some persuading, didn't he, dear?'

Mrs Rees flicked back her hair. 'I wouldn't say that. Although, our chairman is rather keen on his own subject. We did nearly get an expert in French cavalry training—'

'Prussian, dear,' her husband corrected her. 'Eighteenth century equestrian battle formation. That chap from that society that old Lewis always tries to invite.'

'Well, Mrs Christie won,' his wife said.

'Until the next time.' Mr Rees turned back to the steering wheel. The engine revved, and he started out of the railway car park.

Mrs Rees turned to her again. 'We've booked you into the Royal Crown, it's the best there is, well of course, there's the Majestic, but ever since they found mice no one goes there, not now… We'll get you settled in and then pick you up in time for dinner.'

*

There was a bustle of importance at the hotel reception, which was full of elaborate red carpet and carved oak, the polish long since dulled. Now, Agatha found herself in her room.

Her window looked out over a wide street. Through the net curtains she could see municipal buildings, their tall white stone and towering pillars proudly asserting the city's importance.

She remembered Alicia's affection for Wales, her talk of the sea. The street outside seemed solid and dutiful, standing firmly under the heavy sky, its citizens living their everyday working life.

She longed for a sense of being on holiday.

Alicia's card was still in her handbag. She took it out and gazed at it. '*Plymouth Arms Guest House, Penarth.*'

Fifteen minutes on the train from Cardiff, Alicia had said.

She looked out at the threatening clouds. She was glad she'd packed a raincoat.

CHAPTER NINE

'You know the *Carmichael Varieties*?' The woman on the doorstep clapped her hands. 'Here that, Bryn? This lady knows Sian and Madlen and their friends. How wonderful. Come in, come in...'

Janet Parry was smartly dressed, in black court shoes and a well-cut black dress. Her hair was pinned back, and her dark eyes sparkled as she led the way into an airy drawing room.

'Mind you,' she was saying. 'The time they've had. Awful, awful. Two killings, it's been in all the papers here, although at least it's all solved now. Do sit down, Mrs Christie, I'll put the kettle on. She's come from London, Bryn, all the way to Cardiff, imagine, though she's booked into the Royal Crown. Not my choice, I have to say, although perhaps it's improved with the new management...'

There were noises from the next room, a creak of furniture, a heavy step, and then a man appeared in the doorway. He was grey haired, strongly built, in a navy jacket that gave him a military air.

'Here he is, my Bryn.'

'Pleased to meet you,' he said, with a click of his heels, then turned to go.

'Won't you have a cup of tea, dear?'

'Already had a lot of tea,' he said, and ambled away out of the room. There were further scrapings of chairs.

'Poor Cosmina, though I hardly knew her. She was new to the company here. And her partner, I knew him a bit better. Terrible tragedy. Though I do think the newspapers ought to call them man and wife, give them the dignity due to them. Dance partners they're saying, it makes her out to be no better than she ought to be.'

Agatha allowed Mrs Parry to take her coat, and pull out a chair for her at the dining table. 'So they were married,' she said.

'Oh yes,' she said. 'They slipped away one day. That company manager, he was very cross about it. Over in Cardiff they did it, I caught Alexei laying out papers for the register office. "Getting married?" I said, as a joke, but he swore me to secrecy. Said they wanted it kept quiet. Then off they went. Rather a whirlwind arrangement, I thought, but then thinking about it, the company was so unhappy, so many of them had left, and this new manager of theirs, no one trusted him…'

'Georgie Carmichael?'

'Yes, that's the one. So I'm not surprised if Alexei just wanted it all done and dusted, a bit of security in an uncertain world. And he and Georgie nearly came to blows – do you take sugar?'

'No, thank you.' Agatha took the cup of tea she handed her. She turned back to Mrs Parry. 'I heard there was a fight.'

'Sian's partner, Stefan, he's a nice boy, he had to step in. It was something about the bill matter, who was the chaser, I never got to the end of it. But it's like that with trying to make a new company out of an old one, it never works. So many of the old ones had gone,

Madlen had gone off to New York, her poor sister left behind and missing her terribly, lovely girls both of them.'

'You've known them for years?'

'Their mother Lynne and I...' her face shadowed. 'Back in Pontypridd. Best friends since school. Always thought the girls were destined for the theatre, I remember them dancing around their mother's kitchen table. But then, you see, she died, poor Lynne...' She gave a heavy sigh. 'Their father did his best, but he barely lasted another year, his lungs it was, everyone blames the steelworks but you can never tell, my uncle Evan worked there man and boy and he's still going strong... now where was I? Oh, yes, and then they were taken in by their mother's sister. Well, she was a difficult woman, Merwen. Tried to put a stop to their ambitions, all the dancing stopped, all the singing too, it was sad to see. A mean-minded woman, even her parrot was spiteful. Dead now. Not the parrot, her. There was another sister, but she emigrated. It was a shame, they'd have been happier with her. Anyway, where was I? Well, then they ran away. As soon as they could, only fifteen or sixteen the two of them, joined *Tommy's Twinkletoes* at Porthcawl. The family were horrified, but I was delighted. And look how well they've done, to think of Madlen on Broadway itself... Now where was I?'

'Georgie,' Agatha said. 'The fight with Alexei.'

'Ah yes.' She frowned, remembering. 'Well, Georgie was trying to control him, that's what it was, trying to put him in his place. They do that managers, but what did Georgie know? He'd come from running a shadow puppet show. Cardboard cut-outs are easier than real people, that's the problem. And Alexei wasn't having any of it. Stood up to him, see. No wonder Madlen left... I hope she's all right out there. You see, the other aunt, Cicely, the one who emigrated, she ended up in America too. She's dead now too, she died two – no – three years ago, it must be now, we had Doone's Bioscope staying with us, a very learned gentleman, it turned out, knew everything about lizards... where was I? Oh, yes, Cicely, she married a minister from Louisiana, lived very happily from what I gathered...' She picked up the milk jug, peered into it.

'And the argument—'

'What? Oh, Georgie and Alexei, yes. I do remember an odd moment, not long after the fight, they'd all come back here, and Georgie cornered Alexei, in the kitchen here, just the two of them – and he said something about Alexei being stateless, and how he could have him sent back to Russia if he chose. Georgie said he knew all about it, how he'd fled America because he was illegal there, and how he didn't have the right to live in this country either, and Alexei had better remember that it was all thanks to Georgie's tolerance that he was here at all...' She put down the jug.

'And what did Alexei say?'

'Nothing. That's what was so odd. I remember noticing it, as I came into the kitchen, Alexei just standing there, proud as anything, like no one could touch him... More tea? I'll just get some more hot water...'

She bustled into the kitchen, then reappeared. 'It's a long way away, America,' she said. 'That's my worry with Madlen being there. Merwen, her aunt, she lost touch with her sister once she'd gone. Mind you, that was Merwen for you, she invented yet another feud, about money, of all things, Merwen always said that Cicely owed her money, but that was typical of her, inventing grudges. As if a baptist minister's wife is going to have anything to leave to her estranged sister. But that was what she was like, Merwen, choosing to be the injured party. Even the parrot took on the atmosphere of martyrdom… "It's always me, isn't it?" That was one of his sayings. He'd shout it out, "It's always me, isn't it?"' She laughed merrily and Agatha laughed too.

'And then when poor Madlen went off to America, she got caught up in the drama too; Merwen made her promise to track down this money, of course it didn't exist but everything had to be about her, didn't it. Madlen promised her that she'd stay in the States until she'd found out about the money. But of course, her career is going so well there, why would she come back anyway? Anyway, it's over now. No one left to bear grudges. Even the parrot's happier – he was taken in by Teddy at the Pavilion bar, and now they both sing songs from the trenches. *Belgium put the Kibosh on the Kaiser…* you know it? Teddy claims to sing the polite version, but there's another version with some terrible bad language in it, that's the one the parrot sings and he must have got those words from somewhere. More tea?'

Agatha watched as Mrs Parry refilled her cup. The table was laid with a blue cloth, and a vase of daffodils caught the sunlight, flickering with gold.

'So Alexei and Cosmina were married,' Agatha said.

Mrs Parry nodded.

'It's strange, given that everyone said they didn't get on,' Agatha said. She hesitated, then went on, 'And from what you're saying, he needed citizenship here.'

Janet Parry looked up. 'Do you know, I hadn't thought about that.' She stirred her tea. 'But – but Cosmina was foreign too.' She shook her head. 'It wouldn't have got him anywhere, would it? No,' she said. 'What I think, for all that they seemed so ill-suited – I think it was for love. Who are we to say what makes two people fall in love? No, dear, I think the thing about marriage, is that it gives us safety. In this unsafe world.'

Agatha was gazing at the daffodils. 'Although... marriage can't be trusted to be safe,' she said.

Mrs Parry looked at her, and there was a warm sympathy in her brown eyes. 'That's true too,' she said. 'I've always been grateful that my Bryn doesn't ask too much of things.'

'Nonsense.' The voice from the next room was deep and loud. 'My wife is a rare woman,' he boomed. 'Precious as rubies. And every day I give thanks to the Lord that I had the sense to marry her.'

*

The clock on the pier tower struck four. Agatha walked along the wooden boards, watching the waves beyond the curly wrought iron.

94

The brisk wind had blown away the clouds, and fragments of blue sky appeared. She'd taken her leave of Mrs Parry, with a warm handshake, refusing offers of lunch, agreeing to visit again, 'any time you're in Penarth, Mrs Christie...'

There had been no mention of her career as a writer. She wondered whether Mrs Parry had never heard of her, or whether she was so used to celebrity visitors, what with Doone's Bioscope, or the Bentley Boys, that one writer of crime novels was neither here nor there. In any case, it had been a relief to be unknown. Mrs Parry had answered her questions, chatted about the troupe, reminisced about her life in Pontypridd, blushed at her husband's occasional comments, all with great good nature.

The pier was showing posters for the summer season in the Pavilion.

'*Kranko and Kat, illusionists,*' she read. '*Come and see their famous act as Connie the Connemara pony disappears.*'

'*People want to be fooled,*' Luca had said. '*It's all in the mechanics. It's just a question of how you hide it.*'

The mechanics, she thought.

In my work, the murderer is hidden from view and revealed at the end. Is that better or worse than sawing a woman in half, or catching a bullet in your teeth...

Now there's a plot, she found herself thinking, as she walked along the pier, watching the scudding clouds. There was that magician, a few years ago, she remembered the news story, he'd died in some outpost of north London, when the bullet-catching trick had gone wrong and he'd been shot by his assistant…

Too obvious, perhaps, to situate a murder mystery in the realm of illusions.

The clock tower chimed the half hour. It was time to get back to Cardiff and dress for her literary dinner.

CHAPTER TEN

'And all I can really say, to finish…' Agatha stood on the stage, by the lectern, 'is that I still continue to have ideas for my stories, and for that I am grateful.'

She was aware of applause, of the chairman, Dr Michael Lewis getting to his feet, announcing that she would now be taking questions from the floor. Hands were raised, and she answered as best as she could, about where her inspiration came from, did she have a daily routine for writing, 'You seem to know a lot about poisons, Mrs Christie…'

She spoke about the time she'd spent in the pharmacy during the war, how she tended to write anywhere, as long as she had a notebook and a pencil, how she'd always made up stories, even from childhood…

Finally dinner was announced, and Mrs Rees led the way into the banqueting room next door. She found herself seated on the right of Dr Lewis, who refused to believe that she didn't want a glass of wine and placed one firmly down on the table for her. 'Between you and me, Mrs Christie,' he began, as plates of smoked fish were placed before them, 'I'm writing a book.' He poked at the dish in front of him. 'What the devil is this? Mackerel again? I'm sure we ordered salmon…' He looked around for a member of the waiting staff.

'Your book,' Agatha prompted.

'Ah, yes.' He turned back to her. He had a wide moustache, a bald pate, a florid complexion. 'History of the regiment,' he said. 'We lost a lot chaps in the war, don't you know. The wife doesn't believe I'm ever going to finish it. "You and your book," she says. "When are we ever going to have a holiday…" Horseradish,' he said, stabbing a fork at his plate. 'These continental ideas…'

On her right sat another man, a quiet, upright person with greenish eyes and a diffident manner. He was in full evening dress, with a jacket frayed at the cuffs. The removal of the first plates (the chairman's plate entirely scraped clean) gave him an opportunity to lean towards her.

'I'm very pleased to meet you Mrs Christie,' he said. His voice was soft, Welsh and pleasant. 'I'm afraid I haven't read any of your works but my wife greatly enjoys them.'

'I'm glad.'

'She'd have loved to meet you, but she's simply not well enough. This is a rare evening out for me.'

'I'm sorry to hear your wife is ill.'

He sighed. 'It's her lungs. She used to work in the weaving mills up in the valleys. Her sister is with her now—'

'Of course,' boomed the voice at her left, 'it's unusual for a lady to be interested in violent death. I mean, regimental history involves a certain amount of descriptive work about man's inhumanity to man, but for a lady—'

'I'm not interested in violence, Dr Lewis.' She spoke firmly.

'Nonsense, Mrs Christie. I've absolutely no doubt that you'd be first on the scene of a crime, given the chance.'

She took a breath. 'I think – those of us who lived through the war – I think we saw enough of all that. We don't need to dwell on it in our imaginations.'

'I expect you're always viewing dead bodies,' he went on, as if he hadn't heard.

The man on her right spoke up, suddenly bold. 'I think for Mrs Christie's readers, her books aren't about death or violence, but rather the aftermath of both. Certainly as far as my wife is concerned, she finds a humanity in Mrs Christie's stories, and perhaps even an escape from the troubles of this world.' He stopped, as if exhausted.

The chairman was eyeing him. 'Well, Mr Forsyth – if that's your view. But I can't imagine—'

'I think Mr Forsyth has put it very well,' Agatha said.

Dr Lewis pursed his lips, twitched at his moustache, then turned away. 'Ah, here comes the roast beef,' he boomed, getting to his feet to help with the carving.

'I'm sure our chairman's book of battle history will be riveting,' Mr Forsyth said. 'But I have no doubt at all that my wife will continue to read your books, not his.'

He'd smiled, and for a moment she had imagined his wife, her horizons diminished by illness, finding in one of her stories an escape from the confines of her room.

*

And now it was the next day, and she was sitting in the neat, clean breakfast room of the Royal Crown hotel, looking out at the bright morning. Mrs Lloyd, the hotel manager appeared with a pot of tea which she placed in front of her.

'I gather it went very well, your talk,' she said.

Agatha looked up at her and wondered how she knew.

'Mrs Bowen from the Women's Institute was there and she said everyone was very happy with how it had gone. Even Lady McPherson stayed awake, apparently, and she usually snores at the back. I'll bring you some eggs and bacon...' She laid a knife and fork in Agatha's place. 'And the morning papers to read. And after that we'll drop you at the station for the London train.'

Agatha watched the sunlight on the wide windows, listened to the rumble of the city traffic beyond. She imagined herself on the train, heading back to London. She picked up the newspaper, turned the pages. '...*Professor admits guilt in London dancer's death,*' she read. '*Lover drugged, then strangled.*'

The report told in excitable tones the story of how the post-mortem showed that the Romanian dancer had been drugged before she was strangled, and that the professor, previously of good character, had been moved to arrange the death of his rival by allowing a rail to land on him, thereby crushing his skull. '*The accused is due to appear in court later today...*'

She put down the newspaper.

Somewhere in a sitting room in a house in Cardiff, Mrs Forsyth is enjoying the escape afforded by one of my books.

100

That is what I offer my readers. Order, resolution. A beginning, a middle and an end. Clockwork it may be. It may rely on the mechanics. But I am a writer of fiction. A storyteller.

This, she thought, staring at the newspaper, is nothing to do with me. This real life murder, these young people's lives snuffed out, this tragedy…

This is not what I do.

How did I get so caught up in it? However much I count Patrick as a friend, however much I might suspect that there's more to it than this newspaper would have me believe…

It is nothing to do with me.

She gazed out at the spring sunlight. She thought about Penarth, the gracious seaside villas, the holiday sounds of the waves against the shingle beach and the ice cream sellers on the esplanade.

I could take a different train. Back along the coast, to walk along the pier, to stay with Mrs Parry and hear more tales of profane parrots and dancing dogs.

And then what? For how long can I run away?

She pushed away her plate, got to her feet, and went to pack her bag.

*

At the railway station, Mrs Lloyd stood, her hand outstretched, saying her goodbyes. 'Well, do come again. Perhaps the Institute will have you back,' she said. 'They do sometimes allow people a second chance.' With a wave, she got back into her Morris Seven and drove away.

Agatha entered the station, prepared to carry her bag up the stairs towards the platforms. Again, that sense of reluctance, to go back to London, to find herself once more immersed in the drama of Georgie's troupe, of the doubts surrounding Patrick's acceptance of his guilt.

Drugged, she thought. Drugged and strangled.

Of course.

She almost dropped her case, standing, breathless, holding the iron stair rail. An image of Isabella, the night they all first met, insisting on cocktails. Passing a martini glass to Cosmina. '*A few sips*,' she'd said. '*It won't do any harm…*'

'*You know a lot about poisons, Mrs Christie…*'

A martini glass, extended by one woman to her rival.

Would Isabella have gone to such lengths?

'*…A woman who will stop at nothing*,' Georgie had said.

Alexei was married to Cosmina.

Georgie knew about the secret wedding of Alexei and Cosmina. But it seems no one else knew.

And that was another question:

Why would Alexei have married Cosmina? Why then?

She stood by the steps of the railway station, thinking. Then, she turned round and went to the ticket office.

'The London train, madam? It'll be along in five minutes.'

'No, the next one, I mean.'

'Well—' The station master looked doubtful. 'There won't be another for two hours. It's a long wait. And I'm afraid I can't recommend the refreshment room here, though don't tell them I said so.'

She picked up her small bag and headed out into the centre, towards the town hall.

*

'Births marriages or deaths?' The woman at the desk had neat brown hair and a thin efficient face.

'Um – marriages. I think. Although maybe…'

'People usually know what they're looking for when they come here.' The dark eyes were piercing.

'I have a question that needs an answer,' she said.

'And what is your question, madam?'

Agatha sighed. 'I won't know the question until I see the answer,' she said.

The woman's gaze was fixed on her, unblinking. Then she pointed at the end of the corridor. 'All the records are through that door there. The clerk will help you.'

*

Agatha settled at a large desk with a big bound book. 'This is marriages,' the man had said. 'All marriages registered in Cardiff since January this year.'

She flicked through the thick pages. She counted back the weeks. Mrs Parry had said they were there two months ago, so, February, March—

'*Petrovich.*' The name jumped out at her. '*Alexei Fyodor Petrovich. Of Pembroke Gardens, Penarth, Wales. And before that,*

103

East 14th Street, New York. Nationality: Russian. Place of birth: Moscow.'

So, there it was. The two names. The groom. And the bride. *'Occupation: Dancer.'* And there were two witnesses. One gave his name as David Caxton, Occupation: hotel porter. The other was Rhys Miller, taxi driver.

She looked at the signatures. Bride, groom. Two witnesses. She pushed the book away. And all that hope, that sense of a future to end with a drop rail crash-landing on Alexei's head.

The room was high ceilinged, with a hush of leather bindings and the flick of pages.

And now Patrick is due to appear in court. She thought about his admission of guilt, or at least his acceptance of his fate. His belief that the woman he loved was married to a man he hated who had brought about her death.

She stared at the names on the page. The two signatures.

She recalled his look of resignation, as he was led away by the police.

She wondered where he was now. Whether Isabella had stood him bail. Whether she was able to visit him, to give him hope.

She wondered what Isabella really knew.

A flash of memory – the crushed skull, the empty eyes of Alexei as he lay on the stage, a trickle of red his pillow.

Yesterday evening, she had stood onstage, smoothing her grey silk robe, as she talked of plot, of mystery, of hiding the truth until the reveal of the story, the whole evening carried on a platter of polite chatter and bourgeois interest.

What am I doing here? She asked herself. What am I doing here with the clues of a real killing, two real deaths, the work that even now is being pursued perfectly well by the Metropolitan Police?

She closed the marriage register. The heavy noise reverberated around her, and heads were briefly raised from their researches.

I have a novel to write. A murder mystery. A clockwork, unlikely plot about a will. That's what I'm being paid for, and that's what I shall do. Probate, that's what I need to research. Ordinary deaths, people who'd reached the end of their lives, everyday stories of family connections. Like those two cousins, those Irish horse breeders in the newspapers with their disputed inheritance.

Probate.

She went to the clerk, and a few moments later returned to her desk with another large leather-bound register. She began to flick through it. '*The Last Will and Testament of…*'

She idly turned the pages. Those aunts, she thought, the two sisters from Pontypridd, what did Mrs Parry say they were called, Merwen and Cicely. One was a difficult maiden aunt, the other married and emigrated, and the third sister died too young, leaving two girls, Madlen and Sian…

Jenkins.

Here it was. '*Merwen Jenkins. Place of Death, Pontypridd.*

'*I leave my estate to be divided between my nieces, Madlen and Sian Harries.*'

There they were. In black and white, before her eyes. '*I also leave the sum of fifteen shillings to the Hope Endowment for the Study of the True Gospel.*'

Written out in lawyers' ink. A total of a few hundred pounds. A modest legacy. A quiet death.

That's what I need for my story, she thought. An ordinary life. A woman who lives until the age of eighty-one and then dies, leaving her few possessions shared between two nieces and a forgotten gathering of dusty clerics.

She scanned the innocuous wording. An unassuming life which leaves no trace, apart from a few hundred pounds, some memories, and a much happier parrot.

So different from a young woman drugged, then strangled. Or the crushed body of a young male dancer, that fiery, talented young man, felled in his prime by a falling rail, apparently deliberately placed.

And yet, how different death can be.

'*You must be interested in violent death, Mrs Christie,*' Dr Lewis had said.

'*I'm not interested in violence,*' she'd replied.

Here is the trace of an elderly lady, a peaceful death, her few possessions parcelled out between her two nieces. Her eye was caught by the last paragraph: '*...my sister, though deceased, owed me the sum of two thousand pounds, and I write here in my Last Will and Testament that this debt must not go unpaid, even after our deaths...*' A last outpouring of rage. There was even an address of a

106

solicitor in Brooklyn whom she'd appointed to be the guardian of the money should it ever be paid. Hiram J. Beckenbauer, it said.

She leaned back in her chair. Another story, she thought. Another glimpse of character, of family, of narrative. Not violence; just everyday life.

Though I don't suppose I would ever call a character Hiram J. Beckenbauer.

She smiled to herself, closed the probate books. She went back to the marriage section, found the marriage, wrote down the date in her notebook.

What was it Patrick had said to Isabella, about dance being like archaeology? Digging downwards, stumbling upon a treasure, dusting it off…

A different archaeology.

She looked at her watch. She would have to move fast if she was going to catch that train.

*

Half an hour later, she sat on the bench of platform two, waiting for the London train. In her handbag was a copy of the marriage certificate, copied out for her by an expressionless clerk in a measured calligraphy. She'd fled from there, rushed into the post office next door and asked to send a telegram to Inspector Joyce, Scotland Yard.

'Of course, ma'am,' the clerk had said. 'What shall it say?'

Agatha prepared the words. 'Accept kind offer of view of body stop. Research stop.'

The words were taken. The clerk, a short, grey haired man in a stiff white collar, eyed her but said nothing.

'*…I expect you're always viewing dead bodies, Mrs Christie…*'

On this occasion, the chairman of the Driscoll Institute was right.

And even after all that, she was still early for her train.

CHAPTER ELEVEN

Agatha peered down at the clay-grey skin, the eyes not quite shut, now ghostly slits of white.

'You can see the contusions,' the mortuary technician said.

Agatha straightened up, her eyes still fixed on the trolley, the incomprehensible stillness of death.

'Dead bodies,' the technician said. 'Some people can't stand it. As from dust did you come...' His voice was cheery. He flicked his thatch of blond hair away from his round, young face. 'I've always found those words rather comforting.' He looked down at Alexei. 'We'll all end up like this one day.'

'But not having been bashed on the head.'

He tapped his cheek. 'Ah, you're right there, Mrs Christie.' He pointed downwards. 'The bruising's still very clear.'

She could see patches of red on the skin, discoloured into faded blue. She bent to look at his right temple, then his left.

They stood under a strip of bright white light. Beyond them, the chill, clean shelves threw angular shadows.

'He still looks like he did in life,' Agatha said.

The young man looked down again. 'They do, sometimes. Depends how they died. But this was pretty sharpish I'd say. Both the bruises are pretty clear.'

'Both?'

'One where the rail landed, see, on the right-hand side of his head there, and then of course, here, where he hit the floor, there's bruising there too. It's difficult to see, with all this discoloration where the blood has drained downwards.'

'Ah.'

'He wouldn't have suffered. We always say that to the relatives, but in this case it's true. An instant death. And anyway, there aren't any relatives. No one seems to have missed the poor blighter. Only one who cared about him is in the next fridge. And there's nothing to say she'd have missed him either, from what the inspector says.'

Agatha thought about the theatre troupe, their range of responses to the deaths. Stefan with his company loyalty and sense of injustice. Alicia, maternal but professional. Georgie oddly detached, hardly caring at all, although his rage at Alexei seemed to be only just beneath the surface. Sian Harries had been genuinely upset, the only one to shed tears. She had also had that tendency to giggle, Agatha had noted, but perhaps that was nerves, a response to the shock and tragedy of the two killings. And then there was Luca Belotti, who seemed to have only one concern, and that was his own act onstage.

'Seen enough, have we?' The technician interrupted her thoughts.

'Oh, er – yes, of course.' She hesitated, gazing down at the smooth, discoloured face.

'Obviously, there'll be a more detailed report ready for the judiciary,' the technician said.

She turned towards the door. 'Thank you so much,' she said.

110

'Not at all, Mrs Christie. Only too happy to help a writer in their work.' He pulled the sheet over Alexei's face, signalled to a colleague that the body was ready to go back in the fridge.

They walked back side by side to the reception.

'The name's Booth,' he said.

'Oh—'

'For the acknowledgments,' he said. 'Daniel Booth.'

'For—'

'In your novel. That's what people do isn't it?'

'Oh – I'm not sure this will go directly into the next book...'

'Whenever you like, Mrs Christie. I'll look out for it. And here's the inspector – he'd better go in too or there'll be trouble.'

'Trouble, Mr Booth?'

'I was just saying, Inspector, how these writers ought to put the likes of us into the acknowledgements, don't you know?'

Inspector Joyce laughed. 'Mrs Christie here sees no relationship between fact and fiction, she tells me. Despite her extensive knowledge of poisoning...'

'I wanted to ask you,' she began. 'Talking of poisoning.'

Mr Booth doffed his cap and went back into the mortuary.

'What did you want to know?' The inspector paused by the large swing door with its heavy brass rail. He lit a cigar, puffing slowly as it began to glow.

'I gather that Cosmina was drugged and then strangled.'

He gave a nod.

'Do you have any idea about the timing of the drugging?'

He sighed. 'Our tests are inconclusive. The post-mortem showed a sedative had been administered, some kind of opiate, and the strangulation marks concur with this, in that she doesn't appear to have put up much of a fight.'

'She was offered a cocktail,' Agatha said. 'Of which she took a few sips.'

His gaze was sharp. 'A cocktail, you say? When was this?'

'It must have been about twenty minutes before curtain up, maybe half an hour. The girls came to join our party briefly, before they went backstage.'

He took a notebook from his breast pocket and scribbled into it, his cigar balanced at the corner of his lips. 'We have another lead.' He tucked the notebook into his pocket. 'A cup of tea was brought to her in the interval by Mr Belotti,' he said. 'He told us it was his habit to bring tea to some of the cast, and he'd brought a cup to Cosmina. He said he knew that she liked to have three sugars in her "curtain-up cup", as she called it, when usually she took no sugar at all.'

'Mr Belotti?' Agatha considered this.

'It's a question of how long an opiate such as this would take to work. My view is, it would have had to be administered quite late on.'

Agatha gave a nod. 'You mean, not at the start of the performance?'

'She'd have been too sleepy to dance,' he said.

'They were on first, remember,' she said.

'Yes.' His cigar had gone out. He took it from his mouth, studied it. 'That's true,' he said. 'And of course, the problem is, anyone present in the theatre at the time would have had the opportunity to administer the poison, should they have wanted to. Well...' he looked up at her with a brief smile. 'You and I might both have our theories, Mrs Christie. All I can say is, my team is hard at work. We'll have to see what they say.' He held the door open for her. 'I bid you good morning.' He raised his hat and went on his way.

*

She sat on the bus, thinking about poisons. '*People want to be fooled*,' Mr Belotti had said.

Luca Belotti, who had carried a carefully sugared cup of tea to Cosmina's dressing room.

Or was it earlier on, a laughing Isabella, passing her a martini?

The inspector may agree that the fictional world bears no relation to real life. But even real life can turn out to be rather unlikely, with parrots who sing regimental songs and American lawyers called Hiram J. Beckenbauer.

The bus stopped at Piccadilly Circus. She joined the lunchtime crowds, made her way to the theatre. As she walked through the sunlit streets, she was aware of a thought taking shape, a niggling doubt at the back of her mind. A new layer to dig, as Patrick might have said.

She wondered how he was. She hoped they were treating him well.

A man like that, locked away in a cell, with the very real likelihood that he would be charged with murder. To believe he had really killed Alexei, one would have to believe that his passions were capable of carrying him so far that he would want the man dead.

It is not beyond the bounds of possibility, she thought.

*

Georgie was standing in the foyer. 'Mrs Christie. How good to see you. How was the show in Cardiff?'

'It was a literary dinner, Mr Carmichael.'

'It's all show business, Mrs Christie.' He smiled, performed his little two-step dance. She was once again struck by his good humour. 'Full house tonight,' he said. 'Though I might be able to squeeze you in.'

'I don't need tickets for tonight,' she said. 'But there is one thing you might do for me.'

'Oh, and what's that?'

'I wondered if we might go onstage and have a look at the drop rail, and see where Alexei fell.'

He threw her a sharp glance, then seemed to collect himself. 'By all means, Mrs Christie.' His voice was warm. 'Now's a good time, they're all having lunch. Come with me.'

At the stage door he turned to her. 'Research for a book, perhaps?'

She smiled at him. 'Perhaps,' she said.

He gave a bow, opened the door, ushered her through in front of him.

*

'So—' Georgie was gazing upwards into the distant heights of the roof. 'The batten was between those two there, you can see the gap.' He pointed.

Agatha craned her neck, stared into the shadows.

'And Patrick would have had to loosen these ropes here—' He strode to the side. They were alone on the stage, Georgie's voice echoing across the bare boards, into the deserted wings. 'And then, as Alexei was standing – here—' Georgie took up a position just left of the centre stage – 'he'd have let the cords out.' Something caught his eye, and he took a few steps to the back wall. 'Now this—' He appeared holding Luca's ventriloquist's dummy in a ballroom hold, twirled a few steps with it. 'We can use this to show the position of the deceased—'

'Oh no you don't.' The voice was loud, male and London-accented. Luca had appeared from nowhere, and was now crossing the stage, holding out his hands to retrieve his Paco.

'Mrs Christie here wants her re-enactment,' Georgie said, with a broad smile. 'Don't you worry, Belotti, we'll whisk your friend away at the last minute—'

'Is this a joke, Carmichael? Because it ain't a very good one.' Luca was standing, pent with anger.

Georgie stood his ground. Then, after a moment, he handed Paco to Luca.

'Thank you.' Luca was unsmiling, holding the dummy to his chest. 'You want to experiment with death, you can do it yourself.' He turned and crossed the stage.

Georgie stared after him, his face still fixed with rage.

'Mr Carmichael,' Agatha began. 'I'm sure we can get a sense of things without risking any harm to anyone, dummy or not.'

Georgie suddenly strode over to the ropes, unhooked one of them and let go. With a swishing, rushing noise, the drop batten crashed to the floor.

'There,' he said. 'That's where our friend met his end.' He pointed at the middle of the stage.

Agatha gazed downwards at the heavy brass rail which now lay across the wooden boards.

Luca was staring at the rail. He raised his eyes. A glance of pure hatred flashed between the two men.

'Could—' she began, walking around the stage. 'Could the rail have landed any other way?'

Georgie looked at her. He shook his head. 'If he was standing here, poor love… then – no. Look – it came loose just there – and landed bang on there.'

She glanced at the stage, then looked out front towards the stalls.

'It's just—'

'Just what?'

'Nothing,' she said.

Luca had gone to sit on the steps, still cradling his dummy on his lap.

'Well…' She took a step towards the stairs.

Georgie gazed at the fallen rail. 'We are but cogs in the machine,' he said. 'We are but players, acting out our own fragmented

116

destinies. After all, this is real life. It has none of the neatness of make-believe.'

She wondered if she was being teased, but he had stepped towards the fallen rail and was now busy hoisting it back into its ropes.

'There,' he said. 'As if it hasn't happened.' He turned to her and offered his arm. 'Allow me, madam. The steps are treacherous from here.'

She leaned on his arm as he led her down from the stage and into the stalls. Behind them, Luca stroked Paco's head. She glanced back to see him jump to his feet, still cradling the dummy. He walked slowly to the wings, sat Paco back on his chair.

*

Out in the foyer, Agatha turned to Georgie. 'I have another question,' she said.

He was holding the door open for her. 'Madam, I am all ears.'

'When you argued with Alexei – in Wales…'

'Oh, these fights, this temperament, these emotional beings that are dancers…' he gave a theatrical sigh.

'It was about his citizenship,' she said.

His smile died on his lips.

'About the fact he'd come from New York—'

'He'd lied.' Georgie's tone was aggrieved. 'He could have been from anywhere – but it was the pretence that ruffled my feathers, madam. Wasn't it, Sian?' He turned to Sian and Stefan who'd appeared in the foyer. 'Hiram J. Beckenbauer,' he said.

Agatha stared at him. 'Did you say—?'

'Hiram J. Beckenbauer,' Georgie said again, and Sian giggled.

'He'd told me he was American,' Georgie said. 'And then it turned out he'd not managed to sort out the papers. He was stateless.'

'But—' Agatha leaned one arm against the door frame. 'Hiram J. Beckenbauer…? How on earth did you…I mean, that name…' She caught her breath.

Georgie looked at Sian. 'It was her idea.'

Sian laughed. 'It was just a name I'd heard of when I was a kid,' she said. 'It was a joke, wasn't it? Only lawyer I'd ever heard of, and that's just because my aunt would go on about him, back in Pontypridd, how he was in New York, how he would see her right after her sister stole her money or something. It was a joke between me and my sister, going back years. I only suggested it to Alexei 'cos he was the only American lawyer I'd ever heard of. And then it turned out he only knew about wills and couldn't help him anyway.' She gave her little giggle. 'But Mr Carmichael, you were that angry with him, weren't you?'

Georgie's face had clouded. 'He'd told me he was American. And it wasn't true.'

'So—' Agatha was still leaning against the door frame. Her mind was racing. 'So…' she began, turning to him again. 'The question of Alexei's American citizenship was never resolved?'

Georgie gave a shrug. 'Madam, I didn't give tuppence where he'd come from. He could have been from Skegness, from Kazakhstan, from the moon – it was the fact he didn't trust me with the truth.'

'But you kept his secrets,' Agatha said. 'His statelessness. And his wedding.'

Georgie looked at her. His expression darkened. Sian and Stefan also glanced at him, then at each other.

'A wedding?' Stefan began.

'They were married?' Sian stared at her.

'There were rumours,' Stefan said. 'That day they disappeared, do you remember?' he turned to Sian.

Agatha faced Georgie. 'You knew,' she said.

He found his voice. 'A company manager has to keep his children's secrets—'

'You knew?' Sian turned to Georgie.

'But—' Stefan was staring at the boards at his feet, and now raised his eyes to Agatha. 'How did you find out?'

'When I was in Cardiff,' Agatha said. 'I had a look at the register of marriages in the Public Record Office there.'

'Ah, the novelist's taste for research, Mrs Christie.' Georgie smiled with his showman's pretence.

Stefan's gaze was fixed on Agatha. 'But it's still difficult to believe,' he went on. 'Given how much Cosmina hated him.'

Agatha faced them all. 'The thing is – he didn't marry Cosmina. He married Alicia.'

All three of them stood stock still, stunned into silence.

'Alicia...' Sian's voice was a whisper of shock.

'Surely not—' Stefan was frowning.

'Look—' Agatha drew out of her bag the marriage certificate that the clerk had so carefully written out for her.

Georgie snatched at it, read it, showed it to the others.

'Alicia...' Sian whispered, again.

Georgie held the certificate. 'All I knew was that Alexei had told me he'd got married. I assumed—' Georgie's smile had faded altogether – 'I assumed it would have been Cosmina.'

'But – but why?' Sian was pale, her hand resting on the back of a chair.

'Presumably—' Stefan stroked his chin, 'to get the right to stay in this country.'

'But it makes no sense,' Sian said. 'Alicia's made it quite plain she wants to marry Hywel.'

Stefan was standing still and upright, and now gave a graceful turn of his head as realization dawned. 'You mean – now she's free to marry Hywel.'

They all looked at each other.

A hush settled between them.

'What shall we do?' Sian looked at Stefan.

'Do?' Georgie's voice was assertive again. 'Why, dear children, we do nothing. This company is shaky enough at the moment. There is nothing to be done.'

Sian looked at him but said nothing.

'They could both have killed him. Loosened that rail,' Stefan said. 'If they really wanted him out of the way, and they knew suspicion would fall elsewhere.'

'But…' Georgie was frowning, tapping the floor with his foot. 'That man, that friend of Miss Maynard's—'

'Patrick,' Agatha said.

'He was the only one there,' Georgie said.

'This wedding. Who else would know about it?' Stefan looked at Sian. 'Would Madlen know?'

Sian shook her head. 'She'd gone by then. And anyway, she'd have told me.'

'When she comes,' Stefan said. He looked around the group. 'When she gets here, we can ask her.'

Georgie turned to Sian. 'When does that ship of hers dock?'

Sian's face brightened. 'Tonight,' she said.

Georgie made his little dance. 'I have a plan,' he said, and now there was a sparkle in his eyes. 'It has just occurred to me, but it's a very good plan. She should do her act.' He flung his arms wide. 'For one night only. *The Queen of the Trapeze*. I'll get it on the billing. Tomorrow night. Friday night.'

Sian blinked, looked at Stefan. 'She'll be exhausted.'

'It would be wonderful,' Stefan said, looking at her. 'Wouldn't it? You two together. On stage again.'

Sian laughed. 'Typical of you, Mr Carmichael. Thinking only of the show.'

'She'll love it,' Georgie said. 'Won't she?'

Stefan gave a nod. Sian smiled up at him. 'I bet she'll do it,' she said.

They left the doorway, wandered off into the bar. Georgie went to the box office, still talking about trapezes.

Agatha slipped away, back into the theatre.

Luca was alone, standing centre stage.

His body was contorted with grief. He was holding the dummy in his arms. Paco lay limp as a lifeless thing, and Luca was bending over him, his face cracked with pain.

It took a moment for Agatha to realize this was a rehearsal.

Luca stepped this way and that, his body creating a dance of suffering.

He stopped. He straightened up, put down the dummy and walked in a normal, jaunty way over to the wings, where there was a gramophone. He wound it up, placed the needle on the record, returned to his place onstage, picked up the dummy.

A voice began to sing, a male voice.

'There is a garden that I dream of...'

Luca was bending over Paco. He was still, poised on tiptoe. He began to dance, cradling his dummy. The song too, seemed to be expressing all the grief of the world.

'...There love divine, and heaven shall be mine,

In the garden of your heart.'

The music ended. Luca stayed, motionless, a silhouette of sorrow.

Agatha, standing in the shadows, found she had tears in her eyes.

She crept away, back into the wings, pushed the stage door open, found herself on the back stairs.

She stood, breathing.

A song from the war. Words of loss, of love, of grief.

Luca's sorrow had seemed true.

And if that's what acting is – is that what writing is?

To be more true than truth itself.

Patrick is insisting that he is responsible for the death of Alexei. If he was a character of mine, then I could own him. I would be master of his thoughts, his words, his desires.

But he's real. And in that sense, he's nothing to do with me. I can't know what he thinks. I have no idea what he did last Friday, alone onstage, when only Alexei was there.

I have no idea what Isabella is thinking, what she wants, what she believes.

I only know my story. And my own story, my own work in progress, is the one promised to my publishers. It is simple, a murder mystery, in which someone has felt compelled to kill another person.

If I was to write something more true? Something more real? A story of love, and loss. A universal story.

If I were to tell that story, it would start with an Englishman. A man who, in the war, was a soldier, brave and true. A man who, after the war, tried to love a woman.

Tried, and failed.

What was it Isabella had said, about yearning, and art. And husbands.

Agatha leaned her head against the damp brick wall of the backstage stairs.

Archie, she thought. So heroic in war. His restraint, his Britishness, his courage. And yet, in peace, incapable of managing the everyday small challenges of a marriage.

We were both to blame. That's what I tell myself now. Because it makes it easier.

She straightened up, one hand on the old iron hand rail.

But – to be so angry that you want your loved one dead... the way Alexei wanted Cosmina dead.

Perhaps it's different if you're dance partners. One leads, one follows. Total trust in each other.

She sat on the old brick stairs, got out her notebook, found a pencil in her handbag, scribbled a few lines.

A character caught off guard, she thought.

Like the way everyone looked at the very odd news that Alexei had married Alicia.

Clearly no one expected it. They'd expected him to have married Cosmina. Everyone did.

The way Stefan looked at Sian. The way Sian giggled, as if to make light of it.

She put her pencil down. Now, that was very odd. It was almost as if it wasn't a surprise after all—

Of course, she thought.

Of course.

It wasn't the fact he was married. It was who he'd married. It was the name Alicia that was the shock.

She could hear voices coming from the stage. She got to her feet, gently pushed open the door to the stage.

Alicia was standing in the wings. She had armfuls of costumes, and was hanging them on her rail. Then Hywel approached her, and they embraced.

Agatha, still hidden from view, imagined that day in Cardiff. Alexei and Alicia escaping from the company, running to the registry office, saying those marriage vows…

What had Alicia been doing it for? Clearly, not for love. For money? That seemed the most likely. She'd talked of poverty, of how you end up doing anything for money, '*Anything…*' she'd said, with feeling.

And now, watching Hywel taking her hand, gazing into her eyes for a moment – now, she was free. And he, too, was free to make her his own.

The light touch of feet across the stage. Sian ran over to Alicia, embraced her. 'It's all sorted out—'

'She's coming?' Alicia held her hands.

A nod from Sian. 'Tomorrow. My sister.'

Alicia smiled. 'I'll get out her costume. How wonderful,' she said. 'She's really going to do it?'

Sian nodded again. 'We wired to her. She says she can't wait.'

And now Stefan was with them. 'Georgie's over the moon,' he said. 'He's getting the posters printed, "*For one night only…*"'

They laughed, embraced, Stefan and Sian dancing and twirling away across the stage.

Alicia stood, alone now. Over her arm, a Harlequin dance suit in red and black, the long legs brushing the floor. She smoothed it, lovingly.

Agatha, still hiding, had a sense of an approaching finale. She felt a nervous anxiety, a sense of dread.

CHAPTER TWELVE

Mrs Burdett's ranunculuses drooped in the chill of the damp morning.

Agatha stared at the piece of cold toast on her breakfast plate. She picked up a notebook. She flicked through the pages, put it down again.

She stared into space.

This evening, she thought.

What is going to happen?

In her mind, it had all become entwined. Patrick, trapped in a police cell awaiting a court appearance, with his miserable acquiescence in his own guilt. Georgie dancing around the box office, determined to have a full house whatever the circumstances. Sian and her nervous giggle in the face of all this tragedy, awaiting the arrival of her talented sister. Alicia and her secret marriage. Isabella with her moths and her cocktail glass. And Luca, lurking, hostile to Georgie, distant from the company, carrying cups of tea at curtain up; Luca, with his tragic clown, his comedy sawing machine, and now his alienated cityscape, weeping for his dummy who never lived.

And at the heart of it, two deaths. Poor Cosmina, loved by two men, it seems. And Alexei, battered and bruised, crushed, so implausibly, by a falling curtain rail.

And the police so sure they have their man.

It's still so unlikely, Agatha thought.

She got to her feet, picked up her notebook, headed for her study. She settled at the polished table, looked out at her geraniums, a display of red and white, a spark of brightness against the grey of the morning. Carlo must have watered them, she thought.

She opened her notebook, glanced through her writings. '*Marriage and revenge. A legacy*,' she'd written. '*A drowning. A marshland village…*'

Now she picked up her pen and wrote the word '*believable*'.

She stared at the page for a while. Then she wrote '*motivation*'. She closed the notebook.

At her feet lay the bulging file that Carlo had left her. '*Letters from your readers. Awaiting reply*,' the label said. She took the first few letters from the file, settled to a stack of fresh notepaper and began to write. '*Yes, my detective will certainly be returning in a new novel shortly*'… '*No, I hadn't considered writing a novel where the detective is a cat. Such things might be left to someone more able than me*'… '*Thank you for your helpful notes concerning the omnibus routes of London. I thought I had got the numbers right, but I shall certainly check in future*'…

*

At lunchtime, a messenger boy delivered an envelope. 'From Miss Maynard,' he said, waiting. Agatha went to get a few pennies for him. He tipped his hat and ran away down the mews.

Agatha unfurled the creamy paper with its elegant black loops of ink. *'Good news. Patrick has been allowed bail. Bad news – he's coming to the show tonight. Determined, for some reason. I've tried to persuade him to stay quietly at home, but to no avail. I shall be there to look after him. I gather from Georgie you'll be there too. I'm so glad. I fear it will take two of us to keep Patrick from trouble.'*

Agatha gazed at the note. The idea of Patrick being there, of his returning to the scene of the crime, seemed impossible. It added to her sense of foreboding.

She put down Isabella's note and opened her own notebook, staring at the words *'believable'*, *'motivation'*.

The fact is, whatever Isabella has said, she had every reason to want Cosmina dead – and she had the opportunity too.

She thought about the moment when the cocktail glass was handed to Cosmina by a smiling Isabella. The glass was already on the table. Isabella might have just picked it up out of friendliness. But, even if the drink contained a sedative – the cause of death was strangulation. A violent, determined act of murder.

Was Isabella capable of such a thing?

'She's a woman who will stop at nothing,' Georgie had said.

But to go to such lengths?

And, if Isabella had killed Cosmina – what does she make of Patrick's rage? Would she really allow Patrick to continue in this dangerous belief that Alexei killed the woman he loved, to the extent of now being under arrest for killing him in revenge?

She glanced at Isabella's note. Perhaps all this is guilt, this need to protect the man she loves.

Agatha sighed, returned to her notebook. *'A story of marriage and revenge…'*

She put down her pen.

I need a new story.

In her mind, she could see Luca, weeping over his pretend-dead dummy. She heard the song of loss, of love.

My story will be about love, and what happens when it dies. It will be about the sliver of ice in the heart of the artist, about a writer putting his own work before the love of his life.

She thought of Luca, his talent, his stillness, his innocence, the white-faced clown cast adrift against the skyscrapers of New York.

New York, she thought. That brash, thrusting skyline exposed the vulnerability of Luca's innocent clown. New York, she thought. A place of opportunity, of new starts, of Madlen's trapeze act and people called things like Hiram J. Beckenbauer—

She picked up the next reader's letter in Carlo's file. She lay it, unseeing, down on her desk again.

Hiram J. Beckenbauer.

Of course.

Her breathing was quickening with the realization.

That's why it was all so unlikely. That's why none of this story made sense so far.

She got to her feet.

And now, with Mr Beckenbauer, perhaps it will.

She went into the study, picked up the telephone, checking the time, wondering if New York would be awake yet.

'Number, please,' said the operator.

'American service,' Agatha said. The international operator came onto the line, and Agatha explained whom she was trying to call, gave her own number, hung up.

She paced the room, waiting. Across the road, Mrs Burdett had appeared with a small watering can and seemed to be talking to her struggling blooms, shaking an admonishing finger.

Hiram J. Beckenbauer, Brooklyn.

She could hardly breathe.

Her phone rang, loud against her thoughts.

Agatha held the telephone to her ear. There were clicks, silences, more clicks. Then a well-spoken English female voice.

'Connecting you,' the voice said. There were more clicks, and then a young female voice said, in an American accent, 'Beckenbauer and Bosch, may I help you?'

'I'd like to speak to Hiram J. Beckenbauer,' Agatha said.

The American voice was clear and polite. 'Certainly madam. May I ask who's calling?'

'Agatha Christie,' she said.

There was a pause, a click.

'Hiram J. Beckenbauer speaking. And I gather you're Agatha Christie. Are you having me on?' His voice was growling, expansive and American.

'I am that Agatha Christie, yes. The thing is, Mr Beckenbauer, I have some questions for you...'

'I'll tell you now,' came the reply. 'I'll tell you now, the butler did it...'

The conversation was warm, brief and informative. He told her that yes, Mr Petrovich had attempted to consult him. Yes, he'd informed the poor man that he only knew about probate and nothing about citizenship. He'd referred him to a colleague. No, he'd never seen him again, he got the impression that the man had returned to England. Say, are you really Agatha Christie? *The* Agatha Christie?

She reassured him that yes, she was.

'Calling me from London town. Well, whaddya know? And here's me having been no help to you at all.'

'On the contrary,' she said. 'You've been enormously helpful.'

'Well, it's been swell talking to you. I guess whatever reason you had to call me, it must have been important.'

She thanked him, promised him that she would indeed look him up whenever she next came to town, rang off.

She stood in her study, staring at her telephone. She thought about their words flying to and fro across the Atlantic at the speed of light, carrying her thoughts, allowing the truth to begin to settle into place.

*

At five she was to be found, standing in front of her wardrobe, gazing at gowns. She flicked through them, shades of silk, taupe, a pale rose, a pastel blue...

In her mind, she could see Alicia, holding the costume for Madlen's daring act, a slash of red and black against the white-painted backstage wall.

She remembered Alicia's care as she smoothed out the clothes, the wistful, affectionate look on her face.

She thought of Patrick's determination to be there.

She remembered Luca's act, the heartbroken clown alone on the empty stage.

She gathered up her blue dress with a tightening sense of fear.

CHAPTER THIRTEEN

Backstage there was laughter, busy-ness, chatter. Agatha had arrived early at the theatre, had found Sian in the foyer talking to Marie at the box office.

'It's so exciting—' Sian turned to Agatha, grabbed her by the hand, hurried with her through the heavy brown stage door. 'Everyone's talking about it. Madlen will be fifth act, and me and Stef are doing our tango.'

Agatha could see Stefan, in a corner of the stage, practising a turn, a jump, a neat twist of his body as he landed on one foot.

'...we're one act down—' Georgie bustled by. 'Saffra throwing another tantrum, just because I've put Madlen top of the bill, what does she expect, that trapeze act will get them in more than any levitating kid from Margate...'

'Top of the bill,' Sian laughed. 'And billed as star of Broadway too. Saffra will have to put up with it. Stef and I have been put into the first half as it is, and you don't see us throwing a fit of temperament.'

'Troupers, you two. That's the difference. Pure professionals.' Georgie swished past them all, patting Sian on the arm as he went. A moment later he was in the pit, standing with Joe the conductor, pointing at a page of the score. Beyond them the empty stalls, the rows sitting stiffly, awaiting their occupants.

Sian had gone to join Stefan, both now sitting on the floor, stretching their long, dancers' legs.

Agatha walked down the side steps. She could hear Georgie talking to Joe, 'The change to three-four timing there, if we could have it just a bit slower, old son, so when it goes to D sharp...'

She walked along the aisle, out to the foyer.

And there they were, Isabella in a sweeping full-length robe in black and white, Patrick at her side, in bow tie and evening jacket.

'Agatha—' He took her hand. He looked crisp and smart, with a new brightness about him.

'Have they treated you well?' Agatha asked him.

'Given that it seems I have brought about the death of a man, then yes.' He seemed serious, steady and resolved.

Isabella leaned her head against him, with an affectionate smile.

'He can't go far, can you darling?'

'I have to report back to the police station this evening before midnight. And again, tomorrow. Morning and evening, daily. For ever. Or until they get to the bottom of Alexei's death. Which is why I'm here,' he added. He wandered towards the bar, surveying the crowd.

'Oh Agatha.' Isabella took Agatha's arm, gave a despairing sigh. 'He seems to think the clue is in the show. He was determined to come this evening. It's so terribly bad for him...'

'How can the clue be in the show?' Agatha could see Patrick, as he leaned against the bar, scanning the crowd.

'I don't know. He was so sure. "They've got that trapeze act back," he's been saying. Going on about it. "the Welsh girl" he calls her. He says she was there when it all went wrong, when Cosmina met Alexei. He seems to think she'll have the answers.' A flutter of her hands as she watched Patrick, her face etched with concern.

Agatha looked at her. '*How much do you know,*' Agatha wanted to say. '*Under this quivering, feminine sympathy, that core of steel, that makes you so sure you will get what you want—*'

The first bell rang through the hubbub. Patrick was at her side again, offering his arms, one to each. 'Ladies, shall we go in?' He led them towards the door. 'The play's the thing,' he said, with a mirthless smile.

Isabella flashed her an anxious glance, as they went through to the auditorium.

The red velvet seats were now breathing, packed with people. Agatha took her seat, Patrick in between them. Once again, the fading of the lights, the hushing of the audience, as the orchestra played the opening notes and the curtain rose.

Sian and Stefan were as poised as ever, their steps perfectly controlled, their height evenly matched. Agatha marvelled at the power relationship in the dance, the toing and froing of leader and follower. There was a defiance in the stamping steps, in the Spanish music, in the frills of Sian's dress, the tilt of her head with its short spiky hair. Agatha found herself musing on the balance of the dance, how it allowed a play between aggression and harmony.

How unlike a marriage, she thought. Especially, my own. We'd had no fighting, no harsh words, no jagged rocks against which our love had been shipwrecked. It had been in the silences, in the distances, that our love had drained quietly, invisibly away.

She was aware of Isabella sitting on Patrick's other side. She thought about the iron resolve it would take, to love a man who wouldn't return that love.

The tango finished to enthusiastic applause. Then Hywel took the stage, his deep musicality lending itself to expressions of yearning, for his homeland, for lost love, for *an honest heart, a pure heart*.

A short interval. The curtain rose on the New York skyline. Luca the clown, stood, still as a statue, with his melancholy pallor. His grief for Paco eventually gave way to graceful tumbling. At the end the applause was loud and joyful, and continued through to the turn of Saffra the Levitating Persian Queen. Gladys for once appeared to be enjoying herself, and even had a warm smile for Terry at the curtain call.

And then, a sense of hush.

The orchestra struck up a single, sustained chord. A spotlight on the stage illumined the white bar of the trapeze. And there she was. She was slim, her bright red leotard clinging to her slight form, with its zigzags of black along her limbs. She had very long black hair, which swung as she moved. She settled on the trapeze, and began to move gently to and fro with the chords of the music. Then, a syncopated arpeggio – as the trapeze swung higher and higher, with Madlen making a series of acrobatic shapes that became more and more daring. The audience collectively held their breath. The music was discordant and swooping, as she swung by one leg, upside down, or flew into a handstand, letting go altogether, then catching the trapeze as it came back towards her, to gasps from the audience.

Gradually the trapeze began to slow, swinging lower and lower to a point of stillness. Madlen stepped off the bar, took a step towards the front of the stage, and made a deep curtsey, her long hair sleek like a curtain. There was a hush, a moment of silence, and then the audience erupted in applause. A few more curtseys, and then Madlen ran off into the wings as the applause came to a noisy end.

The lights came up.

Isabella breathed out. 'Well,' she said. 'No wonder everyone wants her. And no wonder Georgie was upset to lose her. And look, there he is, with dear Joe the conductor, taking a bow…'

Patrick had stumbled to his feet. 'That woman,' he said. 'I must talk to her. She will know why Cosmina had to die…'

'Patrick – no—' Isabella grabbed his arm, but he shook her off, and headed to the door at the side of the stage.

Isabella glanced at Agatha, and they both hurried after him.

He burst into the wings.

And there they were, both of them, Madlen and Sian, laughing, hugging, laughing again, before Sian ran off to get everyone else. Madlen seemed even more beautiful up close, dark eyed, and porcelain skinned, with a light tinkle of laughter as she was greeted by the company, as Georgie filed in, followed by Alicia, Hywel, Luca and Stefan. Even Gladys and Terry came to meet her.

Patrick's shout interrupted the merriment. 'Miss Harries—' he cried out.

Everyone turned.

'I need to know the truth,' he said. 'I need to know why Cosmina died.'

Madlen faced him, calm, petite – and then she ran to the trapeze, and suddenly the trapeze was lifting, lifting, as she sat tight on the bar, disappearing into the heights of the theatre roof.

There was a silence. Everyone stared into the flies of the stage, in shock and surprise.

'Bring her down.' Patrick addressed the assembled company, who all looked as bewildered as he did, standing dazed with incomprehension. Madlen was so far away as to be out of sight. The trapeze rope swung gently in the wings.

Patrick surveyed the company. He spoke again. 'I am currently facing prosecution for the murder of a man. I am in torment. I admit that I carried out certain actions that might well have brought about his death. I also admit that my motivation was clear, that I believed him to be responsible for the death of a woman that I loved, that I still love.' His voice faltered, then he went on. 'However, over these last few days I have become aware that the story is not so simple, that there are factors that have layered the story with complications. I have been conducting a kind of archaeology, and I am now convinced that the truth lies buried, hidden within deeper strata. It is now my intention to reveal it – or rather, to ask that young woman, now mysteriously having fled from my questioning, to assist me.'

The company all looked from one to another. The trapeze rope still swung, unattended.

It was Agatha's voice that cut through the silence.

'If this is a story,' she said, 'then it is one we must start at the beginning.'

The company, as one, turned to her. Agatha took a step towards Alicia. 'Let's start with you. The fact is, Alicia, when Alexei died, you became a free woman.'

Alicia was standing by her costume rail. She faced Agatha, her face wary, her voice brisk. 'I don't know what you mean.'

'Because, you were now a widow.'

Alicia paled.

'You married Alexei in Cardiff, two months ago.'

'This is all lies,' Alicia said, her voice shaking.

'We've seen the certificate.' It was Georgie who spoke, stepping forward. 'I just don't understand why you hid it from us all.'

Hywel was at Alicia's side, and now he turned to her, astonished. 'You're – you're married?'

Alicia faced him. She looked at his kind, open face, now pale with shock. She tried to speak, but no words came.

'To keep him in the country?' Agatha prompted.

Alicia turned to her with a look of resignation. She breathed out a defeated sigh. She nodded. 'Yes,' she said. 'I married him.'

Hywel was looking at her as if she was a stranger. His voice now cut across the hush of the stage. 'And then he died,' he said.

'Darling—' Alicia turned to him. 'Please try and understand. I was desperate for money. And he offered to pay me.'

'He – paid you?'

'His application to stay in America had failed. He needed to belong somewhere, they were threatening to deport him back to Moscow. He was in fear of what would happen to him there. We organized it in Cardiff... I needed the money. I didn't realize that you and I...' she turned to Hywel, her eyes welling with tears. 'It was a terrible mistake,' she said.

'But—' Hywel said, 'One that was entirely solved by Alexei's death.'

Alicia's expression hardened. She faced him. 'Yes,' she said, her voice level. 'Yes, it was in my interests, our interests, that Alexei was gone. But that doesn't make me a murderer.'

Hywel held her gaze.

Georgie broke the silence. 'My dears,' he began. 'Why the mystery? We all know that the drop batten fell on him and that our friend the professor here was the only person in the room when it happened, indeed, that he's admitted to loosening the cords.'

Patrick was still staring upwards, into the roof. Slowly he focused on Georgie.

'Except—' Agatha said, 'the rail was made to land on him after he'd been left out cold by a punch to his head. There are bruises on both sides of his head, not just one. The rail fell on the left side of his

141

skull. I remembered it clearly, from when we all saw him, lying there.' She gazed at the centre of the stage. 'It's not a sight that would leave one very easily. And yet, when I saw him in the mortuary yesterday morning, the largest contusion was on the right side of his head, a very large blow indeed. You can still see the bruising round the eye. Even the mortuary attendant seemed unsure which side of the head the rail had landed on. All of which led me to conclude that someone must have hit the poor man very hard, and then, when he was already out cold, a second, lethal blow was landed by the rail to the other side of his head.'

It was Patrick's turn to gasp, to stumble. 'You mean...' He turned to Agatha. 'You mean – I knew it. I did have a look at the rope. It's true I wasn't thinking straight. When I went back – it was tempting. And I did think that the rail was unsafe – and I did touch the rope, I admit it all – but—'

'But the murderer was watching you. And it was the murderer who came back and made sure the rail dropped.'

Isabella took a step towards Patrick and grasped his hand. He was immobile, as if unaware of her, staring at the bare boards at his feet.

'Let's go back a bit further,' Agatha said. 'Poor Cosmina. Do we still think Alexei was killed in revenge for killing his partner? Or, is there another story?' She surveyed the gathered company. They stood, motionless, waiting. Georgie had lost his jauntiness. Alicia was pale and shivering, with Hywel holding her arm. And Isabella was helping Patrick to a seat, standing with one hand on his shoulder.

'I'll tell you,' Agatha says. 'Cosmina wasn't Romanian at all. But – isn't theatre wonderful? It can create anything. It can rustle into life a Romanian ballet dancer. It can turn one beautiful young woman into another. Cosmina, it turns out, was a Welsh girl from Pontypridd – in fact, she was none other than Madlen, sister of Sian.'

There was a gasp from the assembled company. Again, everyone gazed upwards. Georgie glanced towards the unsecured rope, which twitched with the movement of the trapeze high above them.

Agatha went on, 'But you'll be telling me, Cosmina is dead. Whereas Madlen is right here, isn't she, sitting up there on her trapeze. Stefan, perhaps you'd do the honours...'

Stefan looked stunned. He faced Agatha, uncomprehending, unmoving. Slowly, he became aware that everyone was watching him, waiting. Slowly, he turned to the rope, took hold of it in both hands and began to lower the trapeze.

The rope creaked and swung.

Gradually the zigzagged black and red appeared, the lithe young body, the long black hair. Her face was expressionless, her dark eyes blank. Agatha walked towards her. She gave a wince, as Agatha reached out and took hold of a handful of hair and pulled.

The long black wig came off in Agatha's hand.

The woman sitting on the trapeze had short, dark hair in a spiky modern style.

'Sian,' Agatha said. 'We should congratulate you. It turns out you've hidden your extraordinary skill as a trapeze artist, which is every bit the equal to your poor dead sister's.'

Everyone was staring at the trapeze. Georgie was pale with shock, standing there wide-eyed. 'Do you mean to say,' he began, 'I could have had that act every night?'

'But—' It was Isabella who spoke. 'I just saw them. Together, the two sisters…'

'The illusions of theatre,' Agatha said. 'Greater than any floating princess,' she said. 'Stefan – would you like to show everyone the wig and the veils that allowed you to look, briefly, from a distance, like Sian, just for those moments before you ran off and came back as you, that little show you both put on just now of two sisters, happily reunited – knowing that we'd all be watching you, a willing audience?'

He faced her, his blank severity now edged with hostility. He said nothing.

'Theatre, you see,' Agatha said. 'We've been entertained with a little play, all carefully staged. Madlen and Cosmina are the same person – and that person is dead.'

Georgie was looking at Sian, who was staring at the floor. He turned to Agatha. 'But how do you know?'

'It's amazing what information is available in the public sphere. I went to the Public Record Office in Cardiff to find out about Alexei's marriage. Once there it occurred to me that I could do my own research, about wills, for my new novel. So, in an idle moment, I looked up the estate of Miss Merwen Jenkins, deceased, aunt of Madlen and Sian. It appeared to show nothing at all, just a rather modest amount to be divided between her two nieces, and a generous

144

donation to a rather odd Christian charity, plus a certain obsessive interest in her sister's trust, administered by a lawyer called Hiram J. Beckenbauer.

'I thought nothing more of dear Mr Beckenbauer until he was mentioned, in passing, in relation to Alexei's American citizenship. There had been this apparently throwaway suggestion from Sian, simply because she'd heard of him through her aunt. It seemed rather odd. Then I remembered the account I'd heard about the other sister, Cicely, who had married a minister and settled in the United States. And I got to thinking about this feud, this disputed amount of money which was apparently quite substantial. Just a story, told me by a gossipy landlady, Mrs Parry, but for some reason it, too, had stuck in my mind.'

She looked around the shadowy space, the eyes of all the company fixed on her. 'Sian and Madlen knew about this money held in trust, that their aunt Merwen was so convinced was owed to her. What they also knew was that, should their aunt Merwen die, this money would be due to them, as claimants on their aunt's estate. They knew about the probate lawyer in Brooklyn who was the trustee.' Again, she looked around the company. 'It might have just stayed for them as a dream, an idea, if it wasn't for two things. Firstly, Madlen got the chance to work in New York. And—' She turned to Stefan. 'And you were determined that the dream should become a reality.'

Stefan's gaze was fixed on her, but he said nothing. Agatha continued, 'I learned today that the probate lawyer, Hiram J. Beckenbauer, did indeed meet Madlen in Brooklyn. He told me he explained to her that the terms of the will were that anyone who claimed the money, now held in trust, had to be a US citizen, resident in New York – apparently to prevent a claim from her spiteful sister. Which left you all with a dilemma. How could either sister claim US citizenship? In the meantime, the new company had formed. Georgie had brought in Alexei, Alicia and Hywel. And you found out that Alexei had US citizenship, or so you thought. So, you hatched another plan: Madlen should pretend to stay in New York, claiming that she was indeed resident and that her American husband was due to join her – but in fact, she should come back here to Britain, in disguise, and marry Alexei, and then, once more herself in New York, would produce him as the American husband and claim the money on behalf of all of you. She kept up the appearance, with frequent messages to Mr Beckenbauer, he told me, as he assumed she was still in New York. You all knew that once everyone was in Wales no one would know if Madlen turned into Cosmina, as Georgie had only just taken on the management with a whole new cast. You persuaded Madlen to join in with the plan, to relinquish her Welshness and pretend to be from Romania, although I fear you were less than informed about such places, and indeed, her accent did seem to slip from time to time, as Isabella said.

'Alexei and Madlen became dancing partners, and you all attempted to get them to marry. But Alexei had no intention of marrying Cosmina, as he thought she was. As Georgie found out, his American citizenship was false, and he was under suspicion of the law there for having faked it. He was keen to leave all that behind him and acquire citizenship here instead, and had offered Alicia money to marry him in order to claim it. That's what he'd asked Hiram J Beckenbauer about, whether such a thing would work, and in fact Mr Beckenbauer told me he'd had to explain he wasn't an expert in immigration law and he'd recommended someone else. So, in Cardiff, two things happened. Alexei disappeared for a day, apparently with Cosmina, and you both assumed he'd married her. And Madlen, posing as Cosmina, allowed you to think that – because she had a scheme of her own. She'd decided to go back to the States on her own, apply for citizenship and claim all the money. She'd already started these proceedings through Mr Beckenbauer, he told me.'

There was a silence, broken by Stefan. 'How do we know any of this is true? How do we know you spoke to the New York lawyer?'

She looked at Stefan. 'You can check with the operator about the transatlantic call I made today. I'm sure they'll have a record of it.' She turned to Sian, who was sitting, head bowed, on the trapeze. 'At some point,' Agatha went on, 'you two must have discovered that this was Madlen's plan. And, enraged by her intention to betray you, you decided on a new plan. Madlen had to be got rid of, and, after a decent interval, you two would go to the States and claim American citizenship instead. And also, believing that Alexei was now her husband and as such having a claim to the money, he had to be dispensed with too. It all fell into place then. No theatricality. No fairy tales. Just ordinary human greed.'

Alicia was holding Hywel's hand. Patrick's eyes were fixed on Agatha, and Isabella was leaning with her head on his shoulder.

'Of course,' Agatha continued, 'the tempestuous relationship between so-called Cosmina and Alexei was fortuitous for your plan. You chose a moment when they were particularly highly strung. You placed a sedative in the tea, the tea that Luca brought her – and then some time after that, Stefan strangled her in the dressing room, where she was found, after the show.'

From the trapeze came a sob, as Sian buried her face in her hands, still swaying slightly to and fro.

Stefan glanced at her, his face expressionless.

'Then,' Agatha went on, 'it was a matter of dispatching Alexei too. And that all seemed very lucky too, when Stefan overheard Patrick's conversation about the loose curtain rail. All he had to do was watch Patrick loosen the rail, in the hope, as you've admitted, Patrick, that it might land on Alexei. Then, after Patrick had left the theatre to join us, you acted. It took a moment for you to appear, hit Alexei hard enough to knock him out, and then let the rail fall and land on him in such a way as to look as if it had killed him.'

Agatha surveyed the party. 'I had been asking myself, why were there bruises on both sides of his face. Until I worked out that this was no coincidence. None of the contrived silliness of the old-fashioned detective story. But just plain old flawed human behaviour – just real life.'

Sian was still was blinking back tears. She looked up at Stefan. 'I told you,' she burst out. 'I told you it wouldn't work…'

'Shut it girl.' His voice was a hiss of rage.

Agatha spoke again. 'It seemed too good to be true – and indeed, it was. I couldn't work out why you both seemed so very shocked at the news that Alicia and Alexei had had a secret wedding. And then I realized that it wasn't the fact that Alexei was married that surprised you, but who he'd married. And at first it suited you very well, the fiction about Madlen being in New York. But to keep your story realistic, you allowed everyone to think that Madlen was about to come back, eventually making it come true. But, as a writer of detective fiction once said, the cleverest killers are often easier to unmask than the stupid ones – they're the ones who are so keen to make the plot work, they take a step too far, so complicating the puzzle that it becomes open to doubt.'

There was a silence. It was Patrick who stepped forward. He looked down at Sian, where she sat on the trapeze. 'You killed the woman I loved,' he said. 'I believed in her. I believed her to be Cosmina, from Romania. I don't care that she was deceiving me. To me she was beautiful, and talented, a light in the darkness. But you killed her. Your own sister. And you almost condemned me to be tried for murder. Do you have anything to say for yourselves?'

Sian was staring at her feet. She reluctantly raised her eyes to Patrick, still swaying on her trapeze. 'It was him,' she whined. 'Don't look at me like that, it was his idea…'

'It was her family. Her damned aunt – her sister—' Stefan raged, his arm twisting around the ropes.

'He was the one wanting the money—'

'She said she'd always hated your sister—'

'He told me to do it—'

'She told me to do it...'

Patrick turned to Agatha. 'At least in your stories,' he said, 'the murderer can be elegant, heroic, warped – wrong, of course, but at least they can have a certain virtue about them. Here we are, with the worst that human beings can be. Mean, avaricious, spiteful, calculating and lacking any kind of morality at all.'

Sian swung sullenly to and fro, her trapeze slippers scuffing against the floor. Stefan glowered, his hands clutched into angry fists at his side.

There was a sudden crash as the door swung open, with a march of feet. Georgie had slipped out, and now appeared with a group of police officers. They moved in formation, a line of five uniformed men, swiftly surrounding the two suspects, and Stefan and Sian were marched out of the door, still blaming each other.

CHAPTER FOURTEEN

It was a warm morning, a week later, as spring gave way to summer and Agatha was writing at the window of her Chelsea home, scribbling fast on the pages in front of her.

The will would turn out to be a fake, she'd realized. The whole plot would hinge on the readiness of the silly widow to be fooled. There would be a structure, a completion. There will be a detective, a central character, and he or she will carry the story, give it its shape.

There was a ring at the doorbell.

Agatha opened the door, aware of a rush of warm summer air, and a large bouquet of flowers, behind which stood Isabella and Patrick.

'For you,' Patrick said.

'We owe you a lot,' Isabella said.

'We thought we'd call on you before we all go to the theatre,' he said.

Isabella pulled at a stray rose leaf. 'Unless we're interrupting…?'

'No, no, of course. Do come in.'

Agatha stood in her kitchen, placing the flowers in a vase of water. Patrick and Isabella hovered in the hallway.

'I'll be a couple of minutes,' she said.

'I can't wait to see what Luca's done now he's on his own.' Isabella talked excitedly. 'And in such a funny little place – Shoreditch? I don't even know where it is.'

'It's a derelict factory site, apparently,' Patrick said. 'He's set it all up. It used to be tile ovens.'

'There—' Agatha emerged from her kitchen. 'I'll just get my coat.'

*

London was drenched in summer evening light. They walked across the bridge together.

'And how is Georgie's company?' Agatha asked.

Patrick and Isabella looked at each other. 'Well—' he began.

Isabella laughed. 'Georgie will always survive,' she said.

'And Sian and Stefan?'

Another glance passed between them. 'Sian and Stefan are still blaming each other, apparently,' Isabella said. 'Sitting in their cells.' She paused by the railings, looked down into the water which glittered gold and pink with the evening. 'Sian says Stefan did the actual killing, which I guess is true.' She glanced up at Patrick.

He gave a shudder. 'One's own sister…'

'And such a complicated plot,' Isabella said. She turned to Agatha. 'As you yourself said, it's the cleverness that gave it away.'

They began to walk again. 'What I can't get over,' Patrick said… He stopped, glanced at the river, looked at Agatha. 'I wanted that man dead. I believed it all to be true, to the extent that I was capable of planning a murder.'

Agatha touched his arm. 'Patrick – it's human nature. We're all capable of vengeful rage.'

'And we're all easily fooled too,' Isabella said. 'As we're no doubt about to find out.'

*

The venue was a tall warehouse building made of old brick. They picked their way across a yard, entered through an industrial doorway.

Inside, all they could see was a vast empty space, a few ladders, some makeshift rows of seats. Through high windows the sky appeared indigo blue.

'Luca says it's about the individual lost in the crowd,' Isabella said. 'He says it's about the innocent clown, the essential solitude of the human condition.'

'It always is with Luca,' Patrick said.

'How is Georgie managing without him?' Agatha asked.

Isabella led them to three of the fold-down chairs. 'Fine,' she said. 'Of course. He says they've got full houses for the end of the run now. He's hired two new acts. Willie and his Whistling Whippet. He's had his eye on him for months, apparently. He wanted a strongman routine—'

'He tried to get Vulcana and Atlas but they're much too grand,' Patrick said.

'So he's settled on a new dance act to replace Sian and Stefan, two rather beautiful young men who throw each other up in the air a lot.'

'So now he's decided that he always preferred dance – "Artistry beats mere muscle," he says.' Patrick laughed.

'Georgie will always make the facts suit his intentions,' Isabella said.

*

They settled in their seats. Others were arriving, murmuring with conversation, finding places. The stage was sparsely lit, and long shadows were cast across its angular space.

'You see?' Patrick said. 'The deserted ruins. Only in this case it's a Victorian factory rather than a Bronze Age temple. But it's still the layers of the past.' He turned to Agatha. 'You should join me on my dig. I'll be travelling to Baghdad. You'd love it.'

'An interest,' Isabella said.

'Like your moths,' Patrick smiled.

'I love my moths. Do you know – ' she turned to Agatha. 'I saw a Lycorea in Regents Park today. Just flying past. Must have come in off a ship.'

'And Baghdad?' Patrick said.

'An opportunity,' Isabella said. 'To fully embrace your status as a single woman at last.'

Agatha smiled. 'I may yet,' she said. 'I need a holiday.'

The audience chattered quietly around them. Patrick leaned back in his seat. 'A moral tale,' he said. 'That poor Welsh girl. And her wicked sister. And a silly old fool completely taken in. I've been asking myself, how could I have been so utterly stupid.'

Isabella touched his sleeve. 'Patrick – it wasn't stupidity. It was your innate goodness, to be trusting, to believe what you found in front of you.'

He shook his head. 'If only that were true. In the end, it was all just a conjuring trick. All done with mirrors. And I was prepared to be fooled.' He turned to Agatha. 'You should write about it, about how often love turns out to be just an illusion. A mirage.'

'But Patrick,' Agatha said. 'What about all the times it's no such thing?'

He was gazing at his hands in his lap. Again, he shook his head.

'Your marriage,' she went on. 'That wasn't a mirage.'

'No,' he agreed. 'Except it's over now.'

'But while it lasted,' Isabella joined in. 'It was a real and true relationship,' she said. 'Like any good marriage.' She turned to Agatha. 'Like yours too, perhaps?'

Agatha hesitated, wondering what to say.

'Just because it came to an end,' Isabella said to her. 'That doesn't make it null and void.'

Agatha met her eyes, aware of a sense of gratitude. 'No,' she agreed. 'I suppose it doesn't.'

'It's just the path that the story takes,' Isabella said. 'None of us can know how it's going to end.'

Agatha leaned back in her seat. 'No,' she said. 'You're right.' She smiled. 'And talking of stories,' she said, 'I had a telephone call two days ago. From Hiram J. Beckenbauer.'

'You did?' Now Isabella was smiling.

Agatha nodded. 'The last bit of the story. He said after my phone call he thought he'd better check the detail about the Jenkins sisters. Up till then he'd had it all on hearsay. So, he went back through the documents, found the sealed envelope that outlined the terms of the trust. And he said, you'll never guess what? That Welsh aunt, Cicely – she died flat broke.'

Patrick looked at her. Isabella looked at Patrick. Patrick began to smile. Isabella laughed. 'You mean...?'

'It's not funny really,' Patrick said.

'The aunt in Pontypridd, Merwen – she got herself into a state about a fortune that proved to be entirely fictitious,' Agatha said.

'And so did those silly girls, and that silly boy,' Isabella said. 'Only, of course, it was all worse than that. Much, much worse. When silliness turns to pure wickedness—'

'A moral tale,' Patrick repeated. He shook his head.

'Hiram J. Beckenbauer insisted I put it into a story. On condition, he said, that I spell his name right.'

They both laughed.

The makeshift auditorium was full, and the houselights began to fade.

Agatha turned her attention to the makeshift stage. The innocence of the clown, she thought. The essential solitude of the human condition.

Well, she thought, I'm on my own. Anything could happen. A new kind of writing. A new name to write under. A holiday. To Europe. Or the Caribbean. Or perhaps, even further afield.

The stage was in darkness. One single spotlight cut through the gloom as Luca walked onto the stage.

Agatha sat back in her fold-up seat, aware of the towering walls around her, the shadows of the industrial past.

A different archaeology.

Perhaps I will go to Baghdad.

ACKNOWLEDGEMENTS

In the Garden of your Heart. A song from the First World War, written by Francis Dorel and Edward Teschemacher.

*

I would like to thank:

The staff of the British Library

Dave Shawyer and all at the British Telecom Archives

Adrienne Gould

Printed in Great Britain
by Amazon

31843930R00088